THE SCENTS OF
MARIE-CLAIRE

Habib Selmi

Translated by
Fadwa Al Qasem

ARABIA BOOKS

First published in 2010 by

ARABIA BOOKS
70 Cadogan Place
London SW1X 9AH
www.hauspublishing.com

Copyright © 2008 by Habib Selmi
First published in Arabic in 2008 as *Rawa'ih Marie Claire*

The moral right of the author has been asserted

English translation copyright © 2010 by Fadwa Al Qasem

A CIP catalogue record for this book is available
from the British Library

ISBN 978 1 906697 23 5

Printed in England by JF Print Ltd, Sparkford

CONDITIONS OF SALE

1

"Did you wash?"

At that time, it was enough for me to nod my head imperceptibly for her to understand what I meant as no one else could. No sooner would I pull out the chair to sit across from her at the breakfast table in the morning than she would ask me this question, in the same tone that had barely changed since she had moved into my apartment.

After that, we said nothing. We became so absorbed with eating our breakfast, it was as if we were participating in an ancient ritual whose details we'd become highly accustomed to as a result of continuous practice. We went through the same motions. We rarely looked at one other for the entire duration of breakfast, but I am certain that Marie-Claire, whose face was round and covered in freckles, was happy. Having breakfast together in the morning, after washing, was one of her favorite things.

Before we lived together, Marie-Claire would rush to the kitchen as soon as she opened her eyes. She would have her breakfast and smoke a cigarette or two as she sipped her coffee. She would then go to the bathroom to wash. She confessed all this to me one day after our friendship had become deeper, more intimate, than before. I expressed surprise; and, little by little, I convinced her to stop this bad habit. "Food is holy; food is a blessing from God," I told her, repeating what my mother always said. "We should be clean when we eat." Within a short period of time, she had become more careful than I to wash before she had anything to eat.

I can see her now, leaning over a slice of toasted bread, spreading a thin layer of butter and then a thicker layer of cherry, peach, grape, or strawberry jam. She dips the slices into hot coffee and milk, then she lifts the slice to her lips, which I never stopped desiring from the moment I met her to the moment she abandoned me.

When she had finished her food, she would pass her fingers slowly over her moist lips, still a little swollen from sleep. "How lovely it is for you to share breakfast with me," she would say, clearly delighted. As she lit her first cigarette she would add, "Do you know that there is nothing better than breakfast?" I would nod in agreement. I, who was born in a house where people did not talk of food except to say that it was a blessing from God. I, who never knew of anything called breakfast in my childhood. If I had happened to eat anything for breakfast, it would have been a piece of hard bread made of wheat or barley, dipped in water for a long time so that I could chew it without risk of breaking any of my teeth, which had taken a long time to emerge. Or I would dip it in yesterday's leftover shakshuka sauce or couscous, which had not gone sour as a result of being left out all night, or whatever was left in the goatskin bag of the buttermilk that had been prepared the day before, or I would eat it with whatever dates or peaches I had stolen.

Marie-Claire would blow out the smoke as she turned her body completely to the open window. She would do so regularly and carefully to keep the smoke away from me, because she knew that I could not bear it in the mornings. She would yawn lazily, and I would catch sight of her gold-covered tooth. Once she finished her cigarette, she would lift her arms, and press her head with her interlocked fingers, revealing her underarms to me.

Ever since then I have become obsessed with looking at women's underarms. Gradually I discovered that these two hollows, which women bear without any embarrassment, are two of the most erogenous parts of their bodies, especially when clean-shaven. When I nuzzle my nose in an armpit and smell its odor, I am overcome by a delicious sensation that reminds me of how I felt as a child when I put my head between the breasts of one of my post-pubescent sisters.

The first time I told Marie-Claire about this she laughed as she arched her brows in astonishment. "You are such a pig. What do you like about underarms, the hair or the smell of sweat?" But for as long as we were together, she always remembered that I adored that part of her body, and whenever she wanted to express her love for me, arouse me, or express her admiration of me for some reason or another, she would fully expose her underarms to me, or she would take my head and push it under one of her arms.

After finishing her meal and smoking her cigarette, Marie-Claire would remain in her seat. During the first few years, I tried to do the same, because I knew that staying near her during these moments gave her a sensation similar to the one she had when we had breakfast together. Marie-Claire would look at the sky. She would do that almost every morning. "Horrible weather," she would say when the sun was hidden behind the clouds. Sometimes I would not be able to control my desire to respond, so I would say, "But the rain, clouds, and wind are beautiful, too."

"You are strange!" she would utter excitedly. "You're not like other people or else how would you consider a sky full of clouds to be beautiful weather?"

I would remain silent as I stared at the spoons and knives. I would collect the crumbs on the table and pour the remaining coffee from the cups into the coffee pot.

When she lowered her head a little and sank into silence, which would happen from time to time, I would seize the opportunity to sneak a look at her. First I would look at her breasts, which always seemed smaller to me than others I had had the opportunity to see. I would look at her shoulders and upper arms, her neck, which, as I later discovered, resembled her mother's in its length and elegance, and her exceptionally soft hands. Then I would gaze at her round face, full of freckles. Sometimes I would try to recall the image that was etched in my mind, or the impression I had had of her, when I saw her for the first time.

I liked Marie-Claire's face. Not because of those lips that I had always desired, and not because her face was particularly beautiful, but because it was round, feminine, and, particularly, because it was comfortable. A mixture of familiarity, spontaneity, tranquillity, and intelligence shone from her face. Sometimes I would look at her face and feel as if I were looking at that of a child, not of a woman over thirty. I also liked it because of the freckles, which made her face somewhat distinctive, and together with the soft blond hair which touched her shoulders, made it more attractive.

At first she would stick her tongue out at me whenever she caught me looking at her. Or she would pout or stretch her neck toward me, bringing her face closer to mine, or she would move her torso away and look at me after stroking her hair in an affected show as if looking at a camera. She would do so as she smiled or laughed. Sometimes she would get up and move toward me. She would cover my eyes with her hands, wrap her arm around my neck, or hold my shoulders and shake me until I confessed that I was a sick man who enjoyed peeping and I promised that I would immediately stop this habit of looking at her in this way, particularly in the moments right after breakfast. Later on she would wave her hand in the air indicating annoyance, shake her head mockingly, or give me a look that she tried to make seem cold and harsh. If she spoke, she would ask me if I had slept well last night, if I was feeling all right, or if I was suffering from anything. Or she would suggest that I cut my toenails, which, as usual, had grown, unnoticed by me, insisting that that would be far better than staring at her face like a repressed man who had never seen the parts of a naked woman's body before.

On days when we were both on holiday, which were few, breakfast would last much longer than I could bear. And because I was afraid of getting bored with sitting down and would then get up, or because I was afraid that my mood would be spoiled, I would turn inward and embark on a journey of memories. I would recall the day my mother had died. I would remember how on that day people loved me as they had never loved me before, and although I did not even know how to kick a ball, as the children of my village repeated mockingly, they allowed me to play alongside their best players and even score many goals. I would also remember that the men allowed me to walk in the wake, something usually strongly forbidden to children my age; and at the cemetery they did not prevent me from watching the full burial rituals. What's more, they gave me the cover with which they had wrapped the coffin to take home with me. As I approached the house yard, all the women who were sitting on the ground to rest after hours of crying and wailing, surrounded and kissed me. That day, during which I was supposed to feel sadness at the loss of my poor mother, I was happier than I had ever been in my life.

Sometimes, when I craved variety, I would not recall the day my mother had died; rather I would try to recall what remained in my memory of my recent dreams. I knew that these remnants intertwined and mingled with each other in a way that added to their mysteriousness and strangeness, but this did not bother me at all. In fact I found it useful sometimes, as it forced me to think of things that would not usually have come to mind had I recalled the dreams completely or separately from one another.

When Marie-Claire sensed that her enjoyment of the morning breakfast had reached its climax and that she had been well compensated for all the mornings in the past when she had not enjoyed having breakfast this way, she would get up without moving the chair, so as not to make a sound, as if she were afraid of spoiling my introverted state of pleasure. Slowly and quietly she would place the cups, small spoons, knives, teapot, sugar, butter and jam containers, and any leftover bread on the tray and carry it to the kitchen. And although she would not turn on the faucet fully, I could hear the water flowing.

She would return after a few moments, carrying a water jug, and turning her back to me, she would start watering the plants, which she made sure were always very near the window so that they would get enough light. After washing up, she would remain in her nightwear: an apron with nothing underneath. Like me, Marie-Claire hated pajamas. She used to say that they reminded her of patients in a hospital. So it was possible, from where I sat, to see the most intimate parts of her body.

I would remain in control; in fact I would usually stop looking at her. I would turn to look at the sky, gaze at the painting on the opposite wall, or return to my introverted state. But sometimes I would get aroused. I would be overcome by a crazy desire to take her as she bent over the plants. I knew very well that Marie-Claire did not like that, because she was not a cow and I was not a bull, as she would say, and because such actions were not suitable, in her view, in the morning. And yet sometimes she would let me, especially when she loved me to water her as she watered the plants—after we drew the curtains, of course.

2

At first I saw her reflection in the mirror opposite my table.

Sometimes I would try to recall the image of her that was imprinted in my mind from the moment I had first laid eyes on her, but I could not. When I raised my head, I saw her. I'm not sure whether she noticed my presence or not. I also don't know when she walked into the café because I didn't sense any movement, nor did I hear anything around me. I must have been engrossed in reading. She, too, must have been careful not to make a sound that would draw attention to herself as she sat down. All I know is that she was sitting directly behind me, within mere inches of my table.

I didn't get a good look at her; maybe that is why I can't recall what she looked like when I first laid eyes on her. I went back to reading. When I raised my head again after a long time, I started paying attention to her. She had changed position and so seemed somehow different to me.

The long straight neck was the first thing that caught my attention; then the freckles that covered her cheeks. Despite all of that, I felt drawn to her round face; and at that moment I noticed, as I looked at her reflection in the mirror, that she had very sexy lips.

I focused my attention on her face. The more I looked at it, the more it attracted me. I guessed from her big smile at the waiter who brought her coffee that she was a regular. She stirred the sugar slowly in the cup and then licked the small spoon for a long time before sipping her coffee with great relish, which was obvious from the way she smacked her lips.

I was sure that she could see me, too, in the mirror that reflected her image. But I wasn't sure if her eyes had fallen on my face, because she was constantly looking toward the street or the café entrance to her right as if she were waiting for someone.

I turned around and leaned my back on the window through which she looked at the street. After a while, I turned back; her face was in full view and her eyes were fixed on me, only to discover her eyes fixed on me. I was not surprised at the time. I smiled at her and she smiled back unaffectedly, or so it seemed. That was when I spoke to her.

The words came out of my mouth, submissively, easily, quickly, as if previously prepared for her. I did not need to build up my courage, which was usually the case when I spoke to women I didn't know. I spoke to her as if I were speaking to someone I had known for a long time. I no longer remember exactly what I said to her, but I am sure it was something like, "I think we've met before somewhere," or "Your face looks familiar to me," or something like that.

She laughed. I am sure she knew, as all women everywhere know, that what I had just said was not true. Her laughter made me happy, and as I looked at her lips to see if they were as sexy in reality as they seemed in the mirror, I saw for the first time that one of her molars was covered with a thin layer of gold. That was the first time I ever saw gold in the mouth of a European, and I found it a little strange. Until then I had not known that they used gold in Europe to treat cavities. I used to think that farmers and rural people where I came from were the only ones to coat their teeth with gold as a sign of wealth, and because they believed that all that shines and glitters is beautiful, especially if made of a precious metal like gold.

I had been in Paris for nine years when I met Marie-Claire at that café opposite the main entrance to the Luxembourg Gardens, which I had entered by sheer coincidence. Five of these years I had spent studying. When I got my PhD, which I was not really excited about, I did not want to go back to Tunisia. I continued working at hotels, which was something I enjoyed because it provided me with everything I needed while also allowing me to lecture as a contract professor at the university whenever they renewed my contract. I was also afraid that if I returned to Tunisia I would remain trapped there for a long time, and that I would suddenly and abruptly be cut off from visiting Paris. That was mainly because they would confiscate the passport of anyone who returned to Tunisia after a long time spent abroad, in order to ensure that their minds had not been tainted and that their love for their country remained true.

I don't know how much time we spent at the café. All I remember is that we were the last to leave. Her laughter encouraged me to move to her table. Actually, I didn't so much move as turn a little to end up facing her fully, and then I slid with my chair toward her.

Because conversations have their own logic, and because no one can direct their course, particularly in such situations, we found ourselves talking about many things. The thread of our conversation would not be cut off, even for a moment. Whenever she was quiet, I would talk, and whenever I was quiet, she would talk. It was as if we had an agreement; as if we were afraid of spoiling or losing what we had if we let silence creep up on us. During that first meeting, and at that café which I had entered by chance, I learned many things about the first real woman in my life.

I learned that Marie-Claire had discontinued her studies of history and geography at Nanterre University without obtaining her degree because she no longer wanted to become a professor as she had once dreamed. She had found employment at the post and communications office in Montparnasse a few months before, after winning a competition for a public posting. She chose to work at the post office because the public sector, unlike the private, guarantees employment for life, and Marie-Claire did not want to find herself unemployed some day. She was, of course, capable of finding another job in the public sector, one that was more relevant to her university studies or the world of books and schools: a librarian, for example. But she chose the post office specifically because she had liked letters, parcels, telegrams, and everything related to the post ever since she was a child.

Her job at the post office did not allow for direct contact with the letters, because her university education meant that she was over-qualified for small tasks such as receiving letters over the counter, delivering them to addressees, or stamping them. But she always found ways to enjoy touching and looking at letters.

She told me about her first days at work: "I would bend over the trolleys that collected all the letters before distribution. I would look at all the different-colored stamps of all sizes. I would contemplate the addresses written in different handwriting. I would stuff my hands into the piles of letters. I would turn them over. Smell them. I do not know why I always imagined that they were carrying happy news. I am always amazed as I think of them traveling in the four directions of the wind; in ships, airplanes, trains and trucks; crossing spaces, seas and oceans, countries, and continents.

"My amazement would grow when I opened one of the bags of letters we received. Some letters arrived worn, creased, and with bent corners; many hands must have handled them during their long journey from one postal center to another.

Sometimes my hands would fall upon letters coming from countries I had never even heard of; in fact, I would even have doubted that they existed on maps had I not read their names on the letters and the stamps. Countries unknown and obscure to me, despite all I have studied of history and geography."

I also learned that she lived alone in what is called a maid's room on the sixth floor of an old building on a small street located between the Pantellion and the Place de la Contre Escarpe—an area frequented by tourists because it is full of restaurants and bars—and that she was happy with her room despite its small size because most of the building's tenants were nice single men and women, or old folk who liked her and smiled at her whenever they met at the entrance or in the elevator.

Marie-Claire also told me that her first two years at university were the best years of her life. During these years, she had met some wonderful young men, some of whom were foreigners from black Africa, Guadeloupe, Martinique, and Algeria. It was also the time when she had read the most beautiful foreign novels and traveled very cheaply to many countries by car because she was satisfied with vegetables, fruits, and canned food, and would sleep in her tent in the open air or in large train stations. I also discovered that Marie-Claire did not like politics or politicians because they were liars and hypocrites, that she despised racism, felt for the Palestinians, and hated violence, terrorism, and all wars.

I learned many other things that I still remember even though they were trivial and irrelevant. For example, I learned that she liked the Touareg and their style of living, and that she dreamed of spending a day with them, riding camels, milking goats, and camel mares, and sleeping in the open desert as the Touareg do; and that she liked paintings and sculptures but did not often go to museums because, in her opinion, they seemed like depressing art cemeteries; that she hated synthetic flowers and could not even bear to touch them; and that she preferred black-and-white photographs.

After we had met many times at this café and several others near the main entrance to the Luxembourg Gardens, I decided to invite her to my place, which was on a street not far from the Place de la Bastille. But when I did, she insisted on inviting me to her place first. I was surprised by her insistence and I still don't know the reason behind it.

Her room was nice and very comfortable. In front of the only wide window stood a tall plant in a large ceramic pot; opposite the plant was a low bed whose headboard was a small table supporting a stereo and whose footboard was a bookshelf stacked with books, bric-a-brac, and small dishes. On the walls, which were painted a yellowish-white, she had hung the works of famous impressionist artists.

She liked my apartment, too. She found it very spacious, especially compared to her own room. And yet, when I suggested she move in with me, after we had been together for several months, during which our relationship had deepened, she hesitated greatly. I believe her attachment to me, which had become obvious during that time, was not enough to convince her to move in with me. I used to wonder sometimes whether she would have been the one to suggest I move in with her had her room been more spacious.

I have to mention here that Marie-Claire's constant presence in my home during the first few months made me so happy that I was afraid the happiness might change into its complete opposite. Never in my whole life had a woman loved me as much as Marie-Claire did. It was the first time in my life that I had lived with a woman in this way. I could see her every day. I could smell her. I could touch her clothes. I could hear her footsteps. I could touch her body. I could inspect her combs, her hair clips, her perfume bottles. I could rummage through her shoes, her handbags. I could watch her take a bath and go to the toilet. I could watch her move her hands. I could watch her yawn. I could watch her get into bed, and get out of bed every morning. I could watch her put on her eyeliner and lipstick, and pluck her eyebrows. I could do all that and much more whenever and wherever I pleased. And I could not believe that this exceptional, beautiful creature was mine, in all her fragility, strength, charm, complexity, peculiarity, contradictions, moods, and whims. Mine and mine alone.

I have to admit that her constant presence near me at home made me nervous, too, especially in the beginning. I was not used to living with women, and I was not familiar with all her likes and dislikes, despite everything she had told me during our café meetings; that and the fact that women change a lot, as it is said. I was afraid of doing something stupid and disappointing her. So I did my very best to be careful about everything I did and to pay attention to everything she did. I would stare long and hard at the toilet bowl to make sure it was clean, and before leaving the bathroom, I would spray deodorizer everywhere. I would put the bottle that I filled with water to wash myself in the corner, so that Marie-Claire could reach and pull off as much toilet paper as she needed without obstruction. I would not leave my shoes in the spot where I took them off as I used to do when I lived alone; instead I would put them where they were supposed to go. I would bathe almost everyday and when I finished I would open the taps to the fullest to let the force of the water wash away all the hair that had fallen from my body. I would change my underwear everyday, something I had never done before. I also abandoned some habits that had a distinct pleasure of their own. I stopped stuffing my finger up my nose;

I stopped burping and farting freely and whenever I wanted. I stopped smacking my lips and blowing my nose loudly. I stopped scratching my skin for fear that she might think I had not washed enough.

I also started listening to everything she said. I would show a clear interest in all her comments. I would respond quickly to her questions. I would agree quickly to her suggestions. I would rush to help her whenever this was needed. I would smile when she smiled. I would not watch television when she was not in the mood for it. And whenever she was tired or complained of a headache, I would remain still and quiet.

I knew that I was being overly cautious. I was sure that Marie-Claire was not so uptight that I had to behave that way and I knew that such things were not important to her. But I made a pact with myself that I would be very careful to avoid doing anything that might drive Marie-Claire to change her opinion of me during that critical stage of our relationship.

Once I was over my feelings of anxiety and tension, I decided to concentrate on resolving an issue to which I had not given much attention until then; in fact I had ignored it despite the fact that it bothered me a great deal: it was the way Marie-Claire pronounced my name. Whenever she called me, I felt as if she were calling someone else. And that hurt.

I spent a great deal of time teaching her to pronounce my name properly. "Mahfouthe not Mafood. Listen carefully, Mahfouthe," I would repeat loudly, trying to utter the letters as accurately and as clearly as possible. I have to admit that Marie-Claire, who was not excited about the whole thing and thought it a bit of a joke at first, made a huge effort during these training sessions to pronounce my name correctly once she realized how important this was to me.

I did not hesitate for an instant to help her throughout the training. Sometimes I would play the role of trainer.

I would not lose my temper. I would not show my irritation. I would remain calm. I would smile at her and praise her whenever she made any noticeable progress. I would describe those damned difficult sounds that refused to slip easily from her mouth. "The letter 'ha' is a very guttural sound," I would explain, before pronouncing it as I held my throat. Marie-Claire would open her mouth. She would stretch her neck and she would try to pronounce the letter. Her face would become red, her eyes would shine, and the veins in her neck would protrude so much that I ended up feeling sorry for her.

She was able to overcome many hurdles, and her pronunciation improved to the extent that it was almost correct sometimes. But she never succeeded in pronouncing my name as it should be. But that no longer hurt; the important thing for me was that, as a result of the great improvement she made in pronouncing my name, it no longer felt like she was calling someone else when she called it out.

Within just a few months of moving in with me, Marie-Claire began to change everything in my apartment. She thought it was nice but she was looking for another kind of beauty; a simpler, more subtle one, particularly in the living room. The first thing she changed was the carpeting in the bedroom, because it was very old; then it was the wallpaper in the living room, because everything about it was depressing—the colors and the flowery pattern, not to mention that it was of poor quality and reminded her of the dismal rooms in common hotels.

She did not need anyone's help, as I had first imagined. She did everything expertly and quickly. She was the one who bought the wallpaper, and cut and pasted it. She chose the style of carpeting, the color, and the number of tiles necessary for the bedroom, and she fitted everything herself.

Later on she changed the curtains because the colors and patterns resembled grandma's curtains, she said jokingly. She put her bookshelf in the middle of the living room to make it look more spacious, because she thought my bookshelf was too big and, besides, it was made of very old wood. She emptied two shelves of her bookshelf to accommodate my books and put the rest of the books, both hers and mine, on my bookshelf, which she moved to the bedroom. She kept the sofa and the table that I had bought from the flea market, but she changed their positions to find a more suitable place for her little table, on top of which she put the stereo. She rearranged the paintings on the wall after adding her own collection of impressionist paintings. As for her plants, she placed them in front of the window, along with the other plants she had bought after she moved in.

She changed other small things to which I had never paid any attention: the toilet seat cover; the mirror, rug, and towel holders in the bathroom; a few light bulbs and side lamps in the bedroom and the living room. She threw out most of the dishes and kitchen utensils and bought new ones.

She was very careful to ask my opinion about everything she did. She always explained things clearly to me, concentrating on her reasoning behind the change. She did not make any change until I had expressed agreement and made her feel, without the shadow of a doubt, that I was convinced of it. She would worry that I had only agreed in order to please her, and that she, who was an intruder to my world, as she put it, would be imposing on me things that I was not particularly excited about.

The truth is that I was not excited about making changes or about leaving things as they were, not because I did not pay enough attention to or care for my home, but because at that time my full attention was focused on Marie-Claire, on her presence that left me little room to think seriously of anything else. But I do have to admit that after all her changes, my apartment did seem much warmer and more intimate than before; it took me several months to become truly aware of that.

3

preferred working nights because I liked the night. When I arrived at the hotel, I was usually energetic and in a good mood. I would have slept during the afternoon and had a two- or three-hour nap before lunch; sleeping in the day did not bother me then. I had become so accustomed to it that when I wasn't working I would spend much of the night tossing and turning in bed or listening to whatever Arabic radio stations I could find.

I liked leaving my apartment when everyone else was returning home. I would take slow walks alone in the city. I would cross many streets, some deserted, with closed shops and cafés, some still bustling with life. Whenever I got tired, I would get on the bus or take the metro and head to Belleville, where the hotel I have worked at for many years is located.

I also liked the nightlife at the hotel. I would sit behind the reception desk opposite the entrance and watch people coming and going; as the night went on fewer people came and went, until, finally, the foot traffic ceased completely. Or I would listen to the radio, daydream, or make up stories from watching the faces of the hotel guests. Other than that, I wouldn't do much. I would receive the guests and bid them farewell. I would respond to their questions and answer the telephone. From time to time I would inspect the hallway and the rooms on one of the floors to make sure everything was in order.

That is why it never occurred to me to work during the day. It also never occurred to me to quit working in hotels, even in the years when I was able to find temporary work as a substitute professor to fill the odd vacancy, which was the best job they had offered me since I had started looking for a position at the university.

But from the moment Marie-Claire moved in with me, I realized that I would not be able to maintain this rhythm, because living with a woman under the same roof requires many changes. For many weeks Marie-Claire said nothing when she saw me leaving the apartment for the hotel. The only thing she was careful about at that time was that I had dinner with her.

Later on she began to insist, more with each passing day, that I stay with her a while longer after dinner. She would find many excuses to support this insistence: "There is a great movie on television tonight," she would say, "and you must watch it with me. I don't like to watch movies alone." Or she would say, "I want you to listen to this new record with me; it is very important for me to hear your opinion of it." Sometimes she would complain of a headache or some other pain, or she would be in a bad mood, which required that I stay by her side for as long as possible.

A few months later she began to complain of isolation. She would do so in a way that sometimes made me feel sorry for her: "The bed is cold without you; at night I reach out for you, I want to touch you, to touch you just to know that you are near me. Sometimes I am so afraid I bundle myself under the covers and hide my head under the pillow and I start thinking of many things to forget my fear so that I can go to sleep, but I stay awake till dawn."

When her complaining started to bother me, I asked her what solutions she could suggest. She answered in the tone of one who has put a great deal of thought into the issue; she said that I should work during the day. Surely I would be able to convince the hotel owner if I wanted to, and she was willing to ask him herself.

I thought a great deal about this; I needed to convince myself first. What made me accept the idea without much discussion was that I was prepared for it. I knew this had been coming; this was the point Marie-Claire had wanted to get to from the moment she had started asking me to stay longer with her after dinner. Also, working during the day would leave me with some free time, contrary to what I had thought earlier. That meant I would not be deprived of the opportunity of lecturing at the university if they asked me to do so.

The hotel owner did not hesitate much in giving me his approval, especially as my Moroccan colleague volunteered to take on my night shift in return for my taking his place occasionally to allow him to spend the evening with his family, particularly during religious holidays and Ramadan.

I was almost certain that the hotel owner would agree to my request, as we enjoyed a good relationship. He had a lot of respect for my behavior, my ideas—despite our age difference—and for my academic knowledge. He was particularly pleased with my work. He was proud that the holder of a doctorate in Arabic literature was working at his hotel; he who knew nothing of the language of his forefathers, as he would always say in French, except what little poetry remained in his memory from his days at the Annaba secondary school before he dropped out to work with his father, and later emigrate to France.

He also favored Tunisians because his maternal grandmother, whom he was very attached to, was of Tunisian origin. Her family had emigrated to eastern Algeria before she was born and settled in Annaba, where work had been more readily available.

I gradually got used to working during the day, discovering that it had its pleasures and advantages. I made sure to return home early, if at all possible, so that I could wait for Marie-Claire. She would enjoy finding me home. As soon as I heard her keys turn in the lock, I would get up and stand behind the door. She would rush toward me screaming in delight. She would hug me tightly and start kissing me as though she had not seen me for many days—a great many kisses, which, with the passage of time and with great difficulty, I learned to regard as mere welcoming kisses free of any sexual connotations.

Once she had stopped kissing me, she would throw her handbag on the sofa or table. Then she would quickly take off her jacket or coat, as though offloading a burden. She would take off her shoes and leave them lying there in the living room. She would create havoc in the order of things and not a little chaos, which I loved, but it never lasted long, because Marie-Claire would later put everything back in its place.

She would sit next to me and ask me many questions. She would ask me what I had done at home in her absence if I had not gone to work. She would ask me what I had prepared for lunch and if it was delicious. She would ask if I had napped after lunch. She would ask me what I read. And if I told her that I went out, she would ask about the places I went to and what I did there.

On days when I worked, she would ask if I faced difficulties going to the hotel or coming back home, and if the bus or metro was crowded. She would ask if I had a good lunch; if there was much work; if any of the hotel guests were foreigners from distant lands—even though I had told her many times that most of the hotel guests were blacks, Arabs, and Turks.

If I did mention something unusual to her, she would cling to me like a child. Her eyes would shine and she would nag me to tell her the whole story from beginning to end, and in great detail. If she noticed that I was not particularly keen to do so, she would cling even tighter. She would hold my hand and repeat her request with more insistence and some begging.

Marie-Claire did not ask these questions to satisfy her curiosity, because of her need to talk, or in order to know what I did in her absence, as I had thought in the beginning, but to show me how much she cared for me. Everything that happened to me, everything I did, was important to her because she loved me.

Sometimes her questions irritated me, and I would wonder at her persistence and unabated excitement. But later I grew used to her; I even began to find comfort in her attention, enjoying it so much that I would feel a little hurt on the few occasions when she did not enquire with her usual enthusiasm.

But Marie-Claire was not satisfied with simply asking her questions and enjoying listening to everything I said; she also made sure to tell me about what she had done herself and what had happened to her during the hours she had spent away from me. She would do so with spontaneity and great care. If she noticed that a certain incident caught my attention, she would tell me about it slowly and accurately, lingering on all the details.

Sometimes I would ensnare her by pretending that something had caught my attention. Marie-Claire would fall easily into my trap. I would nod more often. I would raise my eyebrows. I would open my eyes wide. I would extend my lip. I would do all that, with as much spontaneity as I could muster, to fire her excitement. And when I was certain that she had fallen completely for my game, I would stop making any gestures at all and I would concentrate on her. I would follow the movement of her lips, her arms, her fingers, and her head, while trying hard not to explode with laughter.

Every so often she would express a clear desire to spend the evening out, and even though I was not particularly excited about the idea, I would do whatever I could to comply with her wishes, especially during our first year. I quickly learned that what she called going out was very important to her. "I'm not old yet; I don't suffer from rheumatism or Alzheimer's yet," she would say sarcastically. "I must enjoy life; I want to live."

To Marie-Claire, going out did not mean that we leave home and take a stroll down the streets for a breath of fresh air as we watch the world go by. To her, going out meant that we have a drink at a bar; have dinner at a restaurant; go to the theater; watch a movie; and sometimes all of these things combined if we had the time.

The only thing that bothered me was going to restaurants. To this day I do not understand the collective celebration of food: food should be eaten with modesty, with some measure of decorum, because it is a blessing from God, as my mother always said. I also found restaurants strange places; what was the point of people sitting at dining tables often laid out cheek-by-jowl and then beginning to eat as they stared at one another?!

I used to think that my annoyance at eating in restaurants would diminish or disappear with the passing of time, but it did not. In fact I can say that this feeling grew ever stronger during the few years before Marie-Claire's departure. But I have to mention that going out had its benefits because it made me discover the importance of the cinema, which I have, ever since, admired as much as I admired the poetry of obscure vagrant poets.

4

"What strange coincidence brought us together!! A Parisian born in Minelle Menton and a peasant from a small Tunisian village."

Marie-Claire laughed as she raised her hands to her face to look at her nails, which were painted to match the color on her lips. She was sitting on a chair that she had placed near the closed window. Her feet and arms were bare, to enjoy whatever warm autumn sun entered though the window into the living room. It was clear that she had had a good night's sleep and that she had had her breakfast the way she liked it. Everything about her—the way she moved, the look in her eyes, her laughter, the way she sat in the chair—implied that she was happy and pleased with herself, with me, and with life on that sunny autumn morning.

I pulled up a chair next to her. I sat down and stretched my legs as far as I could so that my feet were almost touching the plant pots.

Marie-Claire leaned toward me and put her head on my shoulder. I leaned toward her a little and, with my eyes closed, inhaled the smell of sleep along with all the other scents that the body emits through the night and that still clung to her even though she had washed.

"You know, when I was born, you were seven years old. Seven years, three months, and nineteen days to be exact."

I decided to remain silent at first; I decided not to divulge what I considered to be secret for reasons I did not understand. Then I felt that this position was not becoming to the woman I loved and slept with, and with whom I shared almost everything; besides the issue was too simple to deserve such secrecy.

"I am not sure that this calculation is correct."

"What do you mean? I know your date of birth very well."

"But I'm not sure that I was actually born on that date. People in rural areas didn't pay much attention to dates of birth in those days. Sometimes they'd forget to record these dates and would only do so much later."

Contrary to what I expected, Marie-Claire was not surprised by this; in fact she said nothing. She came closer to me and pressed her head against my shoulder even more, as if to console me for the negligence I had suffered. After a long silence she asked, "And what did you get up to at that age?"

"Many things."

"Such as?"

"Nothing important."

"I would like you to tell me; I would like to know how you lived as a child."

I did not hesitate much. I responded quickly to her request because the desire to reminisce about these things was overwhelming me, too.

"I used to dig the damp earth with my hands looking for worms. I set traps for quails, larks, and starlings under the olive trees and once I caught them I would grill them over charcoal after plucking their feathers and cutting off their small heads with a rusty shaving blade. I would spice them up with whatever I could get my hands on: salt, cumin, garlic, black pepper. I would steal figs wearing plastic bags or empty tomato cans on my feet so as not to leave any footprints on the sand, to prevent my father, who was obsessed with tracking things down, from discovering that I was the son of a bitch he dreamed of catching and punishing severely so that the figs would be allowed to ripen. I pissed in small holes so that black and yellow scorpions would come out of them. I would chase them as they ran in all directions, moving their tails and trying to find other holes to hide in or rocks to hide under. I would surround them and pour gasoline over them and scorch them, and I would watch them as they struggled and eventually bit themselves and died of their own poison.

"Why did you do that? You are strange!" said Marie-Claire as she raised her head from my shoulder to look at me in astonishment. At that moment I became aware that I really was strange. But I felt no regret at what I had done to those poor scorpions and birds. I did not even feel the urge to say anything to justify or explain myself. All I wanted at that moment was for Marie-Claire to put her head on my shoulder again so that I could enjoy all her scents on that sunny morning. And that was exactly what happened a few moments later, and more. Marie-Claire leaned on me even more so that her underarm was closer to my nose, and to top it all, she took my hand and pushed it between her thighs and squeezed it. It was clear that something was bothering her since she'd said that I was strange. Did she feel that I had been a little harsh? Or perhaps she had done so to encourage me to continue telling her these stories, which helped her imagine my childhood in al-Amayadia village.

"Leave out the scorpions and the worms."

"I would climb the huge olive trees after the picking was over, in search of any olives that remained on the high, hard-to-reach branches or which I could not see for all the leaves and small entwined twigs. I didn't care about the many dangers threatening me should my foot slip a little, should the branch on which I was standing break, or should I lose my balance. The only thing I truly feared was finding myself suddenly face to face with a chameleon because I was afraid of them, and I still am. I cannot even look at one. When I had gathered a bowlful or two of fresh black olives I would trade them with a traveling merchant who came to the village once a week on a mule. He would give me three or four handfuls of cooked, salted, and spiced fava beans or chickpeas. He would fish them out of one of the jugs resting in the wicker baskets, hot, steamy, and smelling delicious. For fear of my father discovering what I had done, I would put the hot fava beans and chickpeas in my pockets and I would run to the fields. I would sit somewhere far away and devour them. I knew that the black round spots all over the skin meant that there were worms inside the fava beans, but I didn't care. I would throw the beans into my mouth without even removing the skins and I would gobble everything until nothing was left. Sometimes it seemed to me that the beans with worms were more delicious than those without.

"I told you to leave out the worms."

"I would look for ant holes. I would choose the biggest and the most crowded. I would attack the ants in different ways. I would pour sand over them, throw sticks at them, or surround the hole with stones. I would amuse myself by watching the poor ants as they ran in every direction to save their lives.

"Leave out the ants, too. I hate ants. Whenever I hear such stories I feel like ants are crawling all over my body."

"At my school, which I hated in all respects—the teachers, the lessons, and many students—I would spend most of my time staring at the ceilings and walls of the halls, trying to imagine all sorts of things and animals from the different-sized cracks everywhere; things such as boats and mountains and foxes and bulls. When I got bored with that, I would think of ways to eat some of the bread in my bag without attracting the teacher's attention, so that he would not do to me what he had done once before. He had approached me smiling, and when I smiled back, he had raised his thick hand suddenly and struck the back of my neck making me spit out the chewed-up bits of bread mixed with saliva all over the faces, books, open notebooks, and clothes of the students sitting next to me. Sometimes I would stare at the faces of students who did not move. They sat looking straight ahead, with their backs straight, arms folded, and heads held high, and I would try to imagine what went on in their minds.

My father believed that school was a waste of time; that was what I used to think, too, from the time I started school until my mother died. "Come here, you son of a bitch," he would sometimes say to me when he saw me getting ready for school in the morning. "Today you'll look after the two cows and the goat." I would nod in agreement. I would throw down my school bag and head straight for the barn. I would drive the herd to pasture and then I would tie the goat to a tree trunk so that it would not run away. But I left the two cows free, and occasionally I would get very close to one of them. I would stand or sit in front of it and watch it move its head and open its mouth to chew the hay. I have liked cows ever since.

"I like cows, too."

"I like their serenity. The way they walk. The way they shoo flies and mosquitoes with their heads and tails. I especially like their nonchalance and carelessness. I thought that all they cared for in the world was to chew grass and lie down to regurgitate it. I also like cows' eyes and udders when they are full of milk. And I like the smell of cow pat . . . ."

"Cow pat? What do you like about the smell of cow pat?"

"I don't know. I like those kinds of smells. That's why I never hesitated for a moment when my mother asked me to fill a rubber basket or two with animal dung for use as fuel instead of timber. The smell of cowpat is not as distasteful as you might think. Do you know what cow pat is made of?

"I don't want to know. Please stop talking about this."

"When the weather got warm, I would swim in the ponds and swamps. In winter when the rains were heavy, the Wad al-Kharub valley would flood, and we could hear the tumbling of the water all the way from the village. I would stop whatever I was doing and run with all the other children toward the valley. Once there, we would take off all our clothes and throw ourselves into the murky waters, without a care for all the uprooted trees and plants, the empty bags, small barrels, old ropes, bicycle tires, bottles, bowls, and dead bugs, snakes, cats, and dogs that the flood dragged along.

In the summer, once everyone had succumbed to sleep, I would leave the house and go to the well, carrying a thick, smooth stick. I knew very well that stray donkeys gathered around the well looking for water at that time, the hottest time of day. I wouldn't be able to quench their thirst because I didn't have a bucket or a rope to get water from the well. All I could do was help the females get some sexual pleasure, believing that this might help them forget their thirst, even if for a little while. Of course I wouldn't do this with all the jennies. I would choose one. I would tie her forelegs so that she couldn't escape, then I would carefully lift her tail. I would touch the stick slowly to the rim of her vagina and then I would insert it all at once."

"Would she respond?"

"At first, she would raise her hindlegs to kick me with her hooves. Then slowly she would get used to the stick. I don't think that the penis of a jack is any softer or gentler than a smooth stick.

"Strange; and what would happen next?"

"Nothing, I would pull the stick out slowly and untie the jenny."

"Would she run away?"

"No, she wouldn't. She would join the herd. Donkeys are strong and patient. They are used to things like that. Did you know that many youth in the village fucked donkeys?"

"Donkeys!! Aren't there any women?"

"Women don't do that until after they're married, and then only with their husbands."

Marie-Claire adjusted the way she was sitting. She yawned lazily and stretched her legs toward the plants. I looked at the nail polish on her toes and noticed that they were painted a color different from that on her fingernails. I quietly freed my hand, which she had pushed between her warm thighs and I crossed my arms as I focused on the plant leaves, which appeared greener bathed in the sunlight. It occurred to me to tell Marie-Claire that I, too, had lusted after a donkey or two before I had the opportunity of traveling to cities and discovering whorehouses; and that I once almost had my way with a jenny who seemed to like that sort of thing because she immediately became accustomed to the stick and started opening her mouth when I inserted it inside her. It also occurred to me to tell her that sometimes I would leave the donkeys to go to an isolated place where I would play with my little tool; but I never found enough courage to do so.

"I didn't always go to the well where the stray donkeys gathered. Sometimes I would take advantage of the fact of my father's succumbing to sleep, and I would sneak into the larder where he kept the plows, shovels, picks, and sickles. I would grab a pick and run to where it was said that my mother had buried a closed lock as advised by the village elders so that death would not strike me as it had done all my siblings born before me. As soon as I got there, I would start digging the earth, in search of the lock.

"Why would you look for it?"

"So that no one would find it and open it."

"And what would happen if someone opened it?"

"I would die."

Marie-Claire did not laugh or smile as I had expected. She took my hand and pushed it between her thighs once again, somewhere closer to her lower belly. I felt a little embarrassed but I did not withdraw my hand even though I was sure that leaving it near such a sensitive place could arouse me, and that was something I was afraid of on that sunny morning.

"I would also go to the burial ground."

"The burial ground! What would you do there?"

"I would look at the graves."

"Weren't you afraid?"

"Of what? I used to believe that the spirits of the dead also slept at that time, just like the spirits of the living. I would sit on some of the graves and read the inscriptions on the tombstones. Or I would go into the small room where they kept the casket and the tiles with which they covered the grave before shoveling the earth over it. One day I circled the casket several times and then I climbed up and lay down on top of it exactly as they laid down the dead and I closed my eyes."

"You lay on top of it?"

"Yes. I remained there for a few long moments. It had a distinct smell: a mixture of wood, the shroud used to wrap the dead, and the aroma of dead people. I wanted to know what the dead felt.

"And what did you feel?"

"Nothing. At first I felt a little fear. I was afraid that I would actually die as I lay there on the coffin."

Marie-Claire laughed. I took the opportunity to remove my hand from between her thighs. Her teeth seemed whiter, and her gold-covered tooth gleamed in the sunlight. I had a great urge to tell her that I found her laughter very exciting at moments like these, but I remained silent for fear that she might once again stuff my hand between her thighs and I would get so aroused I wouldn't be able to control myself.

"And what do you like about graves?"

"Everything. The way they look, the tomb stones, the whiteness."

"I don't like white; it reminds me of hospitals."

"All our graves are white."

"Why?"

"Because no other color suits death like white."

"Graves here are not white, but they are graves like all other graves."

"There is something else I like about graves—the silence. I like the silence of the dead and the solitude of graves. Sometimes I would look for fresh graves. I would bring my ear close to the top of a grave and I would listen for a long time with my eyes closed."

"Did you ever hear anything?"

"Once I thought I heard something—something strange that sounded like a whisper."

Marie-Claire threw me a hidden smile. She looked at me as if to say she did not believe me. She then took my ear in her hand and began stroking my earlobe.

"The plants, I didn't water the plants," she said suddenly as she got up and headed toward the kitchen.

I moved my feet away from the plant pots. I leaned over to expose more of my face to the autumn sun. Then I listened to the sound of water pouring into the jug.

Once she finished watering the plants, she poured a little water in her hand and sprinkled it on the plants with evident pleasure. The transparent droplets slid down the surface of the leaves and fell onto the earth, the sides of the pots, and everything else around them. Some droplets clung to the leaves for a little while before they, too, fell, sometimes audibly, particularly when they fell on the moistened earth.

Marie-Claire caressed all the delicate plant branches with tenderness. She went closer to some of the leaves and gazed at them. She gently removed the dust from their surface with her fingertips. She carefully removed dead or yellowed leaves. She immersed her fingers in the soil to see how moist it was. Sometimes she would get closer to the plants just to smell them.

I watched her movements with admiration mixed with a little bewilderment. At that time I could not understand her great attachment to plants, which, in the end, were nothing more than a bunch of leaves, branches, and tiny stalks without meaning or value. I did not understand all the attention she paid to those plants and her daily efforts to water, prune, and clean them.

Sometimes this bewilderment grew to the extent that it almost matched the bafflement I felt at the care and attention people paid to cats, and, in particular, to dogs that urinated and defecated on the sidewalks in front of everyone. I must admit that I was lucky because Marie-Claire, whom I loved and lived with, did not like cats, dogs, miniature rabbits, guinea pigs, or the hamsters that had started to invade households. The only things that she made sure we had in the house were plants.

Marie-Claire put the empty water jug on the table without taking her eyes off the plants; it was as if she wanted to make sure that she had done all that she could for them and that everything was in order. She then came back to her seat. She stretched her bare feet so that her apron receded up her legs, revealing more of her thighs. She took hold of my earlobe again and began stroking it. I did not move my head, nor did I move my ear away from her hand; I knew that Marie-Claire greatly enjoyed fondling me like that.

"At that age, I almost died."

Marie-Claire stopped caressing my earlobe. She withdrew her hand, put it on her thigh, and looked at me in confusion.

"I got a very serious disease."

"What was it?"

"I'm not exactly sure, but when I got older and asked about it, everyone told me I got sick from the sun!"

Marie-Claire put her head against mine; she wrapped her arm around my shoulder, and I was enveloped in the aroma of her underarm.

"One day I woke up later than usual. It was summer. I remember very clearly that I ate three big peaches. I also remember that when I woke up I had been sleeping in an area fully exposed to the sun and that my forehead was hot. I felt very weak. After a while I could no longer stand. I collapsed on the floor and started vomiting. It was the most danger-ous sickness I had ever had in my life. It lasted over three months, during which time I lost a lot of weight and a lot of hair, and I became so weak that I lay on my side or my back almost all the time. Upon my mother's pleading, I was carried to a doctor who came every Thursday to Makhaleef, the village nearest to ours. After a month of medication, I hadn't got noticeably better, so everyone gave up hope for my recovery except my mother. She didn't abandon me for a second. From time to time my father would make fun of her or accuse her for neglecting household chores to look after me. What was strange was that this disease showed me that my father did not hate me as I had believed, and that he loved me despite the harshness that he, like all other fathers in the village, thought necessary for my upbringing.

"I was alone when he entered the room. I'm not sure where my mother was at the time. I was terrified when I saw him standing before me. When he came closer and leaned over me, I moved my head away and stared at his eyes. He smiled at me, and my fear lessened, but I remained cautious and ready to protect my face with my arms. I was surprised when he put his head on my shoulder and then his thick hand on the back of my neck with a tenderness I was not accustomed to. We stayed like that for several, seemingly endless, moments. We didn't move. We didn't say a word.

"He smiled again when he raised his head and moved away. He put his hand in his pocket as he looked at my face. He took out one of the broken alarm clocks that he kept in a cupboard that only he was allowed to open and handed it to me, saying, 'Take it, it's yours, play with it and don't give it back to me.'

"That broken clock was my first present. Later on, when my mother died, he gave me another broken clock. And just a few weeks before he himself died he gave me a third."

"And what did you do with all those clocks?"

"I used to play with them and then I sold them piece by piece."

"Sold them? To whom?"

"To other kids."

"And what did you sell exactly?"

"The winders, the hands, the wheels, the screws, the winding springs."

"Would you sell them for much?"

"That depended on the piece. Sometimes I would not sell, but barter. Once I gave a child a large clock hand in return for a snake."

"A snake?"

"Yes, a snake that his father had killed. It was long and missing only a small part of its tail!"

"And what did you do with a dead snake?"

"I would play with it. I used it to scare kids I did not like and to defend myself."

"How long did you keep it?"

"A few days. I only threw it away when it began to rot."

"Where did you keep it?"

"In a hole no one knew about except me. When I needed it, I would take it out."

Marie-Claire moved her head away from mine and removed her arm from around my shoulder. She adjusted the way she was sitting and pulled her apron toward her knees, covering what was visible of her thighs. At that moment I became aware for the first time that the stories I told her were a little exaggerated. I never attempted to exaggerate the events. I tried to be as accurate as possible, but I was aware that I could have told them differently had I been completely free of this hidden desire to impress her, which overwhelmed me, I am not sure how.

As I was wondering if it was useful to continue telling these tales, Marie-Claire looked at me in a way that made it clear that she was still happy with herself, with me, and with life on that sunny autumn morning. She took my hand, saying as she got up, " Forget the snakes now. Come help me change the sheets."

5

I heard the sound of her quick footsteps on the wooden floor, then the door opening and closing, and then her footsteps again on the wooden staircase. I waited a while because I was afraid she would suddenly come back to the apartment, which happened sometimes, because she had forgotten her umbrella, a book to read on the metro, or her cell phone. When I was certain that she was not coming back, I got out of bed.

I was awake long before the alarm clock went off. I saw Marie-Claire reach out to switch on the little lamp near the bed and press the button to switch off the alarm, as she always did when she had to wake up and get out of bed before I did. I closed my eyes. I remained still, pretending to be fast asleep.

I heard her yawn. I felt the bed move as she stretched. Then I felt her come close and lean over me. Usually that would make me happy, and I would drag myself toward her to feel the warmth of her body and take in the scent of her sleep. But this time I remained quiet. I did not move at all, even when she leaned over me with her shoulder and raised her arm so that I felt my nose in her armpit.

It was obvious that Marie-Claire wanted to say something to me before she went to the post office. I was certain it was something of the type that she imagined would make me forget what had happened the day before. But that was exactly what I sought to avoid that morning. That was exactly what I was afraid of because I felt ashamed of myself and embarrassed before her; and I was afraid that this feeling of pain, which had disrupted my sleep all night, would grow.

I can still see Marie-Claire's face. I can see her eyes glistening with desire. I can see her quivering lips, a little swollen from all the kissing. Fingers moving and invading every inch. Breasts rising and falling. Heartbeat getting faster, the hot face redder; the hot body, which could no longer wait, writhing with desire.

Suddenly she looked at me with eyes half-closed. She smiled at me in a way that suggested she did not expect anything more of me that night. She turned her back to me. Her naked body seemed more beautiful than before. I fixed my eyes on her body as though I wanted to possess it simply by looking at it. Her body returned to its usual rhythm. It cooled down slowly, slowly, until it become nothing but a mound of flesh. I felt ashamed of myself. I felt that I could no longer look at it. I quickly turned to face the opposite direction and switched off the light.

That was the first and last time I failed to enter her. What was strange was that it should have happened after the long period of instruction during which Marie-Claire had taught me many things that had helped me discover energies and secrets of the body that I had never known existed; things that I had paid little attention to but which now seem vital to me. She made me aware of the incredibly sensitive spots on her body. She taught me how to arouse her. She taught me how to make use of my fingers; how to move my tongue inside her mouth; how to use it to lick her breasts; how to caress her with the palm of my hand. But the most important and vital thing I learned during that critical stage of our relationship was how to control my desire: how to hold on for as long as possible, not giving in quickly, so that Marie-Claire could also get her share of pleasure. I must admit that I suffered a great deal, and I endured much pain in order to control myself because Marie-Claire, unlike the few women I had known, took a long time to climax.

At first I would wonder if Marie-Claire was like all other women. I would do my very best to do whatever I knew pleased her. Most of the time this would take so long that I would end up too tired even to move. I would wipe my brow as I panted and then I would collapse on the bed for a while to recover.

Marie-Claire would not be upset. On the contrary, she would become more affectionate and gentle. She would plant little kisses on my forehead and cheek. "Don't worry my little one," she would say in almost a whisper as she toyed with my nose. She would get up, go to the kitchen, and bring me an apple or a pear. She would peel it and feed it to me. "Eat, my little one," she would say. She would sit directly opposite me, her legs raised and open, scandalously revealing all her most intimate parts. She would not feel embarrassed when she caught me staring occasionally, taking advantage of this opportunity, which had never been offered to me before by other women. Contrary to what I believed, she did this spontaneously, without intention to arouse me, because she believed that it was only normal that she should not hide any part of herself, no matter how private, as long as she loved me.

She would smile whenever our eyes met. "It is as if you have never seen this before," she would say somewhat bewildered. I would remain quiet and then I would turn away in embarrassment. She would also go quiet. Many long moments later she would start to kiss me and caress my body. "Come, don't be afraid. It's just a question of training and habit. Come, everything will be just fine." I would recover my strength and try again.

My eyes slowly got used to the darkness. I lifted my head from the pillow and looked at her. I saw her body, which had turned into a black blob. I concluded from whatever I could see of her that she had not moved; that she was still naked and huddled exactly as she had been when I had switched off the light.

Was she still awake? I was not fooled by the silence surrounding her. I knew that it was deceptive; she was capable of remaining still for a long time. I leaned my head toward her and listened carefully. I heard her rhythmic breathing, but I was not convinced that she had fallen asleep until several moments had passed.

I got a sudden strong urge to see her face and hands, because I might have discovered from the way she pursed her lips or opened her mouth, or in the form of her hands and fingers, the position of her head on the pillow, or other such things, something that might alleviate these painful feelings, which would not let me sleep.

I didn't move. I remained motionless. It was impossible to see her features or even her hands in all the darkness, even if I were to get out of bed and move to the opposite side, which she faced, to look at her directly. Besides the lights in the room, which I did not consider switching on because I did not want to wake her, the only way I could see her face and hands was to open the curtains a little to let in the street light.

I hesitated a great deal before getting out of bed very carefully. I approached the window but grew so apprehensive that I was unable to do what I had intended to do. The desire that I had felt when still in bed to touch her back had become so strong that I began to doubt the point of looking at a sleeping face by street light, in search of something I was not sure I would find.

I went back to bed and drew closer to her. Without looking at her I extended an open palm and glued it to her body. I realized, from feeling the slight indentation of her spine, that my hand had landed on the exact spot between her lower back and the top of her hips. Every now and again I moved my fingers a little and then I would stop. When I realized that these fleeting touches did not wake her, I moved to other areas of her back and shoulders. I noticed soon that these small movements eased my anxiety, even calming me a little.

I went on making these slow movements. Suddenly I realized that I had fallen asleep. I was not sure for how long, but I sensed that it was for quite a while. I discovered as I looked around in the darkness, now seemingly less all-enveloping than before, that Marie-Claire had changed her position. She was now sleeping on her other side, facing me, her face mere inches from mine. I also discovered that my hand, which had been roaming over her back, was now under her neck.

I, too, turned to sleep on my side, without withdrawing my hand. My knees touched hers; they were cold. I pulled the covers to cover us both. I moved closer to warm her cold body, oblivious this time to what she might say or do were she to suddenly wake up.

I closed my eyes and I could see Marie-Claire again with her glimmering eyes, her swollen lips, and her fingers trembling with desire. I clung tighter to her body, as if to protect myself from her haunting image. A short while later I removed my hand from beneath her neck; I got out of bed and went to the living room.

I sat on the sofa for a while after switching the lights on. I looked at the paintings on the opposite wall. I paced from kitchen to living room and back again for a long time. I looked out the window to the empty street without moving the curtains. The street was empty that late at night except for a few fast-moving taxis. I leaned over the plants. I picked up some fallen leaves. I looked at them for a while, then rubbed them together and threw them in the pot. When I went back to the bedroom I noticed that Marie-Claire had changed her position again. She was now on her back, with her arms and legs spread out. I lay down beside her. I remained still because she had left me barely enough space. I fell asleep and woke up repeatedly until the alarm went off.

6

arie-Claire stretched out her arms. She moved them in the air as if trying to get hold of something unseeable. She had lain down on the only sofa in the small living room. Her legs were slightly raised; her feet were bare, and, as usual, they were touching the sofa's armrest. Her head was buried in a pillow the color of her hair, which was wrapped in a bun.

From time to time she closed her eyes or yawned loudly as she looked toward the wall on which she had hung a large, colored painting of *The Kiss* by Gustav Klimt, whom she greatly admired. For a long time she neither spoke nor moved, so that it seemed to me that she was sleeping, which happened sometimes, especially when she came back exhausted from the post office. But she moved her arms again in the air and said quietly, as if speaking to herself, "I love Minelle Menton."

I was sitting at a side table near the window, with the curtains still open, even though night had tightened its grip on the city sometime ago. I was thinking of the vagrant poetry I had read a few hours ago, and I was wondering if it would be a good idea to focus on the vagrant poets in the lecture I was giving my students the next day.

"When I stroll through Minelle Menton, I feel as if I am not in Paris, but in a village."

I leaned on the window and peered outside, where everything was engulfed in darkness. I could not see anything. When the darkness was less thick, I would be able to distinguish the top of the sole tree standing where the street-lights did not reach. A huge plane tree in the backyard of an old building, surrounded on all sides by more buildings. Sometimes I would think how lucky that tree was, as I contemplated the parts of it that were not hidden from view by the gray buildings. They did not cut it down as they had surely cut all the other trees. They left it to grow big enough for me to enjoy seeing it reflect the changing of the seasons, and so that it could become a sanctuary for birds escaping the noise of the city and the fumes of the cars.

"Did you know that Minelle Menton was not annexed to Paris until recently? In 1860 to be exact. Before that, it was just a village separated from Paris by huge fields where sheep and cows grazed."

I focused my gaze toward the tree again, hoping that once my eyes had became accustomed to the darkness, I would be able to see it. When I was sure that this was not going to happen, I closed the curtains and, without getting up, pushed myself and the side table over the smooth wooden floor to the center of the living room. Marie-Claire turned to lie on her side with her back to the wall on which Klimt's painting hung, making it possible for me to see all of her face. It seemed to me, in the soft light, that her face was pale and devoid of that mixture of calmness, intelligence, familiarity, and spontaneity; nonetheless, I found it comforting as usual.

"I spent the first ten years of my childhood in Minelle Menton. We lived in an apartment on the second floor of an old building. Its huge wooden door did not open easily; a strong push or pull was needed in order to enter or leave the building. The stairs were wooden, almost entirely covered by carpeting in the center, to reduce the sounds of creaking and the sound of shoes on wooden floors. There was a small elevator that barely fit two people, and only if they were very thin. It was used by the elderly and some of the residents on the fifth and last floor of the building. The nicest thing about the elevator, in my opinion, was the mirror: it was long and completely covered the wall opposite the door. Sometimes I would get in the elevator and shut the door without pressing any buttons, and I would turn around slowly to look at myself."

Marie-Claire let out a sudden, loud laugh that I had not expected in her state of calmness, weariness, and relaxation. I laughed, too, and I stared at her shaking bosom; then I slid with the side table toward the sofa to be closer to her.

"Can you imagine that I used to find myself pretty? And the more I looked in the mirror, the more I was convinced of that. The strange thing is that I only find myself pretty in the reflections of elevator mirrors; that's why I liked them.

She laughed again, but not as loudly this time. Her eyes shone, and her face regained some of that combination of tranquillity, spontaneity, and intelligence.

"Sometimes, when there was less movement in the building, I would spend a lot of time in the elevator, and when I heard a sound or felt some movement, I would reach out to press one of the buttons. No one imagined that I would go into the elevator to look at myself in the mirror. It would not occur to anyone. And when someone managed to enter the elevator, I would immediately turn my back to the mirror and pretend to be thinking of something important, or I would say something to give the impression that I hadn't pressed the right button.

"In the elevator of that old building, and in front of the mirror I loved, I became aware for the first time that I had many freckles. It was there that I began to examine these small spots spread all over my face and arms. I hadn't paid them any attention before then. I had never even questioned the reason for their existence or what they might mean.

"From that moment on, I developed a complex and became depressed on account of those freckles. I would hide whenever I could and I would cry in silence until my anger dissipated. I didn't understand how it was possible to make fun of people for something they couldn't help.

"Later, as I got older and began mixing with adults, I was able to get rid of this complex, for I discovered that men did not hate freckles; in fact some men liked them, especially on the face."

Marie-Claire passed her hand over her head. She toyed for a moment with her hair, which was in a bun; then she let it fall free so that strands of it fell over one of her shoulders. I was not able to see the freckles on her face, even though I had come closer because of the weak light. Even so, I found her more beautiful and attractive once she had freed her hair from the bun, which I felt did not suit her because it emphasized and bared her neck, making it seem very long.

"The building was at the end of a narrow street, like many streets in Minelle Menton. Most of its inhabitants were French of humble background, such as ours, Moroccans and Sephardic Jews, pied-noirs, and Arab immigrants. Sometimes disputes would arise and fights would break out between the street's inhabitants: between the pied-noirs and the Arabs; between the Moroccan Jews and the French; between the Sephardic Jews and the pied-noirs. But it rarely developed into more than swearing and cursing. Others would intervene quickly and put an end to the dispute before it got worse.

"I remember only one violent fight. I remember it well because someone almost got killed. It erupted for a simple reason, as was rumored later on, between an Arab and a pied-noir fruit and vegetable seller. I didn't see how it started. When

I passed by the fruit and vegetable store, as I did every day on my way back from school, the fight had already started. They were both grabbing each other, and as each one attempted to slap the other, each also attempted to throw the other to the ground. It was obvious that they were tired. But neither of them wanted to stop fighting. The pied-noir's face was red from excitement and fatigue. Blood was pouring from the Arab's mouth and nose, staining his clothes and dripping onto his shoes, which, I still remember, were white. What was strange was that people didn't make any serious attempts to put an end to the fight. They made mild attempts to separate them or asked them to stop hitting each other. Then they would leave, or move back and watch. I stood far away and I, too, started to watch. I was scared, but I could not move. I was rooted to my place, as though it were the first time I had seen such a violent fight.

"Suddenly, something that no one had expected happened. In the blink of an eye, there was a flicker of a knife blade followed by a sharp cry. I saw the seller stagger a little and then fall full body to the ground, pulling a few boxes of vegetables and fruits with him. The Arab began to look around him in horror. When he saw that people turned their faces away when he looked at them or moved back in fear, he threw the knife to the ground and took off running. Luckily the seller did not die; the stab to his right side was superficial and the wound only flesh deep."

As I listened to Marie-Claire, it occurred to me that I had never seen a murdered person before in my life. I had seen many dead people: my mother, then my uncle, my father, my aunt, my maternal uncle, my maternal aunt, and her daughter. I had grown up around death. Hardly a year had passed without my hearing the sound of wailing here or there. I was the last in line. I came into this world too late, and the moment I started to become aware of my surroundings, a whole generation of relatives had already grown old and gray, and the angel of death began to visit them one after the other. I had also seen many funerals, but I had never seen someone who'd been murdered.

I realized after a while that I had to rid myself of this thought. It was not appropriate to think of murder and the like when I should have been happy, like Marie-Claire, that the poor man had escaped death, for she would probably have suffered a great shock had he died. I tried very hard to free myself of this thought, but in vain. As I was wondering if concentrating on the thought a while longer, as opposed to trying to get rid of it quickly, would be a better way to get it out of my mind, Marie-Claire changed the subject.

"The street was not quiet, even though it was small and narrow. Most of the time it was full of people and cars; even so, I used to love it. I liked that mix of sounds, languages, scents, and colors. I liked all of its cafés, restaurants, and shops. It was then that the couscous restaurants began to shoot up, as well as the eastern sweetshops, and that was also when butchers started writing 'Halal Meat' on their signboards. And it was then that I ate qurn al-gazal and dates stuffed with almond paste for the first time in my life.

"My father worked as a waiter at a café that was only a few steps from our building. Those who did not know him very well called him 'Monsieur Maurice,' but his friends and café regulars would teasingly call him 'the ambassador,' because he considered looking elegant in front of others very important. He would insist on wearing a necktie to the café, picking the right one carefully to make sure it matched his clothes. He greased his hair with hair oil and slicked it back with a comb he always kept in his back pocket. He would carefully make a straight parting in his hair. Do you know Charles Tourneur? My father always used to remind me of him, although he didn't really resemble him, either in his features or in his mannerisms.

"He loved life; he had a great appetite for it. He loved all the little pleasures and delights it offered. Food, sweets, women, fun and games, joking, cars, good wine, holidays, weddings, birthdays, dance parties, horse races. My mother used to say that he had inherited this from my grandfather, who had died a few months before I was born."

Marie-Claire became quiet and, despite everything I had just heard, I was surprised to realize that the thought that I had never seen a murdered person before was still prominent in my mind. So much so, that I had a strong urge to ask Marie-Claire if she had ever seen anyone run over by a car, shot by a bullet, or who had fallen from the sixth or seventh floor of a building, and risk her anger at being asked such a strange question when she was talking about Minelle Menton, the neighborhood she loved more than any other in Paris. I resisted the urge. I leaned against Marie-Claire and began nodding and smiling to keep her talking.

"My father was very attached to the countryside, like most people of his generation and social status. He was proud to be a true Frenchman, as he used to say. He liked rugby and enjoyed drinking wine; he would cut cheese and sausages with a small penknife he always kept in his pocket. But he mingled with everyone: Jews, Arabs, Polish, pied-noirs, and blacks. Occasionally he liked to repeat the few Arabic words he had learned in Algeria, where he had spent two years as a soldier in the topographical segment of the army.

"During those years I was greatly infatuated with him. I don't think I ever loved anyone the way I loved him. He also loved me so much that I imagined that my mother felt a quiet pain, even a little jealousy, because of this love, particularly as I was their first and only child.

"I used to go to bed early and wake up early so that I could be with him as soon as he got out of bed. Mornings were the best. I would stand in front of his bedroom, and as soon as he opened the door and came out, I would rush toward him. He would take me in his arms. I would encircle his upper body with my arms and legs, burying my head in his chest, not caring about the prickly hair that grew there.

"I can see him now as he stood in the bathroom in front of the mirror, his tall, somewhat plump body upright; he used to like mirrors, too. His arms bare, his belly protruding, his suspenders dangling. He put soap on his cheeks. He would dip the brush in hot water and make enough lather to cover his entire beard. Then he would start to shave as he whistled or hummed bits of his favorite songs.

"When he sat at the table for breakfast I would always sit next to him. I would do nothing but eat. He would be the one to pour milk and a little coffee in my cup for me. He would put in the sugar and stir it for me. He would cut the bread into thin slices and spread it with butter and jam. 'Open your mouth princess,' he would say to me as he fed me each slice. 'Eat slowly so you don't stain your clothes.'

"During vacations and on days off from school, he would sometimes allow me to go with him to the café where he worked. The café owner, 'the Pole,' as they called him, and the waiters would greet me with great warmth and give me whatever drinks and foods I desired. I would stand behind the counter so that I could watch them as they worked, or I would sit at a table in a remote corner to watch the café visitors or the crowded street. It was there that I discovered early on the world of cafés, and I have been in love with that world ever since.

"One time we went to the café by car. And because he was afraid that people would mock him for using it to travel a distance of no more than a few meters, we drove around Minelle Menton, we crossed the entire Boulevard Belleville, and then we headed back to the street where we lived. But instead of parking the car opposite our building as usual, he parked it in front of the café so that he could see it as he worked. I remember that it was an old, red Chevrolet. He loved cars and greatly enjoyed driving them.

"As Sunday approached, he would grow happier, not because he didn't have to work on that day, but because we were going to travel by car to the nearby village where my mother now lives. We had bought a small house there years ago. Going there every once in a while to refurbish and repair the place so that it would be ready for the day we moved in was a good excuse to take the car for a long drive."

Marie-Claire let out a long yawn as she moved her extended arms in a way that reminded me of the exercises we used to do during physical education classes at school. I glanced at the clock on the bookshelf only to be surprised by how quickly time had passed; it was already past midnight. I needed to go to sleep because I started work early the next day and had to get enough sleep so that my lecture about the vagrant poets, which I was heavily relying on, would be exceptional. That way I could prove to the students who argued with me, or even criticized me at times, that I was qualified and that I deserved to be their teacher. Yes. I had to go to bed. But I remained right where I was; I was afraid that Marie-Claire would accuse me of being selfish, and that she would reproach me harshly for leaving her at the most critical of moments.

"When my father died, it had been many years since I had left the family home to start a new life on my own, yet I cried bitterly over him. I was so devastated by his death that I started to wonder if our connection went beyond the normal father–daughter relationship. His image remained with me for a long time, in my waking hours and in my dreams. And what made the pain worse was that I was alone at that time; there was no man in my life. What's more, I was pessimistic and depressed after a failed romance with a fellow student who studied at the same college."

I was sure that she was about to cry at any moment. I waited a while, looking around the living room in order not to embarrass her, but Marie-Claire did not cry. She slowly reclined on her back again, returning to her earlier position. She then threw me a quick glance, smiling to let me know that she had decided to forget her father's death and the pain it had caused. I was overwhelmed with relief, and I, too, smiled as I turned toward the clock, moving my head so that she would notice it was time to sleep. But Marie-Claire paid no attention to any of my gestures.

"At the Pole's café I was to meet the first person I had ever loved in my life; can you guess who it was? Ladislaus, the café owner's troublesome son. Sometimes I think that had it not been for my father allowing me to go with him to the café I would not have had this delicious experience, especially at a time when I was such an introvert and had a complex about the freckles on my face.

"He was beautiful then, like most Slavic people. I don't know what became of him later. I haven't seen him since we moved to Le Marais, where my father found a job as a driver for a rich Jewish woman, which made him promptly quit his job at the Pole's café. I loved Ladislaus more than he loved me. But he was braver than I was, and, I have to admit, also smarter. I was infatuated with the way he spoke and with his powers of persuasion.

"'Come,' he would say to me, as soon as his father and the waiter left us to attend to their work. 'Come, I will show you something beautiful.' This was always the way our meetings went at the café. I would not hesitate for an instant. I would follow him with my little heart pounding because I was sure that something was about to happen to us. He would turn around and go down the open metal stairs. I would do the same. 'Go down slowly,' he would call to me loudly, as if afraid that I could not hear him. 'Hold on tight to the railing. Don't move your foot until the other foot is safely on the next step.' I used to love hearing him say that to me; the more excitedly he spoke, the deeper my happiness.

"We would go down to the basement, where every corner was piled high with boxes of various colors containing full and empty bottles of wine, beer, soft drinks, bags of potatoes, and onions. Cooked and salted legs of pork, garlic bulbs, and frying pans of various sizes hung from the ceiling. He would hold my hand, and my heart would beat faster still. We would move to one of the corners carefully, cautiously, so that our feet didn't stumble over whatever pots, cans, and beer barrels were scattered on the floor. 'Help me,' he would say as he bent over a bag of potatoes or a box filled with beer bottles. We would move it a little, looking for the traps his father had set in various places, which he would change regularly so that the mice would not get accustomed to their position and learn to avoid them.

"We rarely found an empty trap; the basement was full of mice. If the mouse was alive, we would release it from the trap and set it free. We would do so carefully and quickly to avoid getting caught. Once, we released a small mouse and put it on the floor, but instead of scurrying away, it just stood there. We pushed it a little toward the sacks of potatoes and onions, but it wouldn't budge. We didn't notice until then that the poor mouse was so weak it couldn't even move. Suddenly we heard the door creaking open. Ladislaus swiftly picked up the mouse and hid it in his pocket. When he took it out of his pocket once we were sure no one was coming down to the basement, it was a lifeless body.

"In that basement, and a few moments after the mouse died, a man kissed me on the lips for the first time in my life. It was a long kiss that did not surprise me, as I'd been waiting for it. What surprised me at the time was that I did not find it as enjoyable as I had heard a first kiss should be. In fact, I felt a little annoyed because I didn't know what I was supposed to do when Ladislaus stuck his lips, wet with saliva, to mine. Was I supposed to play with his lips, too? And more particularly, was I supposed to move my lips when he moved his? Or was I supposed to remain still and surrender to him?

"From that moment on, Ladislaus would kiss me whenever we were alone in the basement. After the second kiss, I began enjoying his kisses, and the more he kissed me, the more I loved him. As for Ladislaus, his courage would push him further than that. He would put his hand under my skirt, and he would slide his fingers on my thighs, breasts, or lower back, but his courage did not extend to touching my more sensitive regions."

I felt a jealousy of Ladislaus growing inside me. Ladislaus, who was the first to enjoy Marie-Claire's lips, which were her most delicious feature. For the first time I felt that some of what she recounted really affected me, although it had happened so long ago. In an effort to overcome this feeling, which I was not able to bear at the time, I repeated to myself some of the verses of the poetry of al-Uhaymir al-Sa‘di, the vagrant poet and thief who had run away to the wilderness and wastelands for fear of death. I tried to imagine him keeping company with snakes and wolves and eating bitter cucumber stems.

"I did not return to Minelle Menton until many years later. I found it almost exactly as I had left it. The street where we had once lived had not changed much. The owners of the shops, restaurants, and cafés were the ones who had changed. As for the residents, they were still Jews, Arab immigrants, pied-noirs, and humble French people. I asked about the Pole at the café, which had seen me fall in love for the first time, and they told me he had left Paris with his family to live in Montargis, where he had bought a luxurious hotel."

My leg felt numb so I got up. I remained still for a very long while. Then I looked at Marie-Claire's face. Her eyes were now shut. Her arms were crossed over the top of her bosom. Her voice, which had lost most of its strength a while ago, was now more akin to a whisper. Her words came out slowly, stumbling off her tongue.

"I stood in front of the counter and ordered coffee or tea; I can't remember which now. The basement door was ajar, and I was not far from it. From time to time I would move closer to the basement entrance and stick my head inside to take a peek, but I saw nothing. It was too dark. The only thing I could see was the top of the staircase."

I walked toward the window and parted the curtains a little. I looked long and hard at the buildings, searching for the tip of the plane tree. I thought of al-Uhaymir al-Sa'di again as I stared into the heavy darkness, without being able to pinpoint any image of him in my mind.

When I closed the curtains, I heard Marie-Claire's even breathing, signaling that her body had finally surrendered to sleep. It occurred to me to wake her up so that we could retire to the bedroom, but after some hesitation, I decided to leave her there on the sofa, for she was as fast asleep as a little child.

7

Young Ladislaus was the cause of our first fight.

"How could you leave me sleeping on the sofa?" Marie-Claire asked me.

There was no anger in her voice. Yet her question, which I had not expected at all, upset me—especially as it was the first thing she said to me when I got up in the morning.

"So that you could be alone all night with your lover, Ladislaus."

I don't know how these words tumbled out of my mouth. It was as if someone else was talking for me. I had no doubt that my jealousy of Ladislaus was greater than I had originally imagined. It was clear that the vagrant poetry which I had read before going to sleep had had no effect at all.

"Aha, so you are the jealous type."

She smiled and went to the kitchen to prepare breakfast, which we had in silence for the first time. Later on we left the apartment together, and once we reached the metro station, we parted. She headed to the post office and I, to the university.

Throughout that day I couldn't forget what I'd said to her. As soon as the lecture was over, which went well this time because the students really enjoyed the vagrant poets, as I had predicted, I knew that I'd made a mistake when I'd replied that way to her question, which, after all, was just a normal question. Even worse was the fact that I had proved myself to be a weak, fragile man, who was jealous of a child who used to kiss her more than twenty years ago in a café basement filled with mice.

I thought of apologizing to her as soon as she got home. But I quickly decided against it, despite my deep regret at what I had done, not only because I found it hard to apologize then, but also because I wanted to push her to do something similar. I wanted her to make some sort of mistake, too: to shout at me, for example, or reproach me harshly. And why not! To curse me, even though I doubted she would. And so my feelings of regret faded as I gradually forgot the impression of fraility and weakness that I had made on her.

Everything I planned and prepared myself for fell by the wayside, however. This first and relatively insignificant fight made me realize that, when it came to things such as this, Marie-Claire was no different from all other women. Despite the combination of innocence, familiarity, and tranquillity that radiated from her face and sometimes made me feel as though I were confronting a child, Marie-Claire possessed devastating weapons, ones that would never occur to you, the most dangerous and the most torturous of all to the human soul being silence.

As soon as I heard the key turning in the lock I jumped to my feet. She kissed me as usual, but she did not hug me. She flopped onto the sofa in such a way as to make it clear that she was tried from work. I watched her take off her shoes and jacket as I waited for her usual questions. But she remained silent.

I left her alone in the living room to rest a while. I returned to find her a lifeless body on the sofa. After hesitating I decided to broach the subject.

"Angry?"

She didn't reply. She clasped her hands behind her head and closed her eyes.

I repeated the question. She opened her eyes. She looked at me for a while then closed her eyes.

"Why don't you say something?"

"I have nothing to say."

"Are you tired?"

She shook her head.

"Then why are you so quiet?"

"I don't know."

"You don't know? You must be angry."

"I'm not angry, but!"

"But what?"

"I don't know."

"How can you not know? I want to know."

"It's not important."

I was so overcome with agitation that I lost control.

"What did I say to make you so angry? You are too sensitive; you are a strange woman."

I suddenly realized that I had entangled myself even more. I felt even greater regret and I berated myself. I got up and went to the kitchen. After a few long moments I returned to the living room. I sat down next to her and, changing the subject, said, "Do you know how the lecture at the university went today?"

She moved her head slightly without saying a word.

"Peacefully. I felt the students' respect for the first time. Do you know why?"

I waited for a word or a nod, but none came.

"Because I spoke to them about the vagrants."

That was the first time I had ever mentioned the word 'vagrants' in front of Marie-Claire. I said it in Arabic. She looked at me with eyes betraying a desire to speak, but she remained silent. Later, when we had ended our fight, she expressed a great interest in the vagrant poets. I told her about them and translated some of their poetry for her; she liked them a great deal and would ask me about them from time to time.

"Do you know who the vagrant poets are?"

I asked her with exaggerated excitement as I moved closer, trying to pique her interest as much as possible.

"Poets and thieves. Yes. Poets and thieves at the same time."

She looked me in the face, her desire to speak getting much stronger. I seized the opportunity and added in the same tone of excitement, "And bandits, too."

I was silent for a while. Then I went on quietly as though revealing a secret, "And criminals."

Now I gazed at her face. Her lips parted and shivered slightly. I imagined that she was about to smile. A reassuring sensation took over me and I went on, "And outlaws, too. That is why they used to live in the wastelands and the wilderness with wolves and snakes."

I realized all of a sudden that I had nothing more to add about the vagrants at that critical moment when it seemed to me that Marie-Claire was beginning to thaw. Without thinking too much I continued telling her what I had told my students.

"Al-Uhaymir al-Sa'di reached a level no one before him had ever reached. He was comforted by the howling of wolves, and whenever he heard a human voice he would run away in fear."

Marie-Claire turned to face the window. She extended her arms and stuffed her hands between her thighs, but I did not lose the hope that I could push her to speak and end this silence that I could no longer bear. I was certain that she was itching to say something after all I had told her, even though she pretended the opposite. This time, I spent some time thinking before I decided to tell her about al-Saleek bin al-Salaka, because I had noticed that the students liked him more than all the others.

"Al-Saleek, who was black; no one knew the wilderness like he did because he kept returning to it."

Marie-Claire looked at me again for a moment, then closed her eyes.

"He ran so fast he could outrun horses."

Suddenly she got up quickly. She bent over the plants. She touched some of the leaves. She began contemplating them with total disregard for what I was saying. I gave up and stopped talking. I lay down on the bed in the bedroom for a while, then I went to the kitchen to take the plates to the living room table to prepare for dinner time, which was fast approaching. Except for the few words she uttered at the beginning, Marie-Claire did no more that evening than move her head to look at me from time to time.

Marie-Claire did not change her behavior for three days. She would kiss me in the mornings when we separated and in the evenings when we met. We would sit together in the living room, and we would have dinner together, but she spoke to me only when necessary and with as few words as possible. When, on the fourth day, I asked her for the reason behind this strange silence she replied without anger or excitement, "In future don't do these idiotic things again."

8

grabbed her pillow, covered my head with it, and closed my eyes.

As soon as I woke up, I turned to hold her, but she was not there. The pillow was cold, but her place under the covers was still warm

I went to work without having seen or touched her, without having smelled the aroma of her sleep. I did not feel her as she yawned, leaned over me, or kissed me. I did not feel her get out of bed, close the door, prepare breakfast, and turn the key in the lock. She must have done everything so quietly so as not to deprive me of the deep delicious slumber in which I had surely been immersed.

I did not get out of bed, not only because I did not have work that morning, but also because I was afraid of spoiling that sense of exhilaration, should I get up. I tossed about in bed a little and then turned to lie on my back. Her pillow was now directly over my nose. It had a strong aroma, part perfume, part sweat: the scent of a sleeping woman, delicious and intoxicating. It added to the feeling of exhilaration enveloping me. I passed my nose slowly over the pillow, looking for the point where the aroma was concentrated. I pressed on the pillow a little with my left hand so that it would not slip, and I started sniffing it as I felt her place, which was still warm, with the fingers of my other hand.

Before that night, I could never have imagined that women could be so generous.

It was as if my body had been reborn; I felt it discarding everything that had tied it down and held it back. All the deprivation accumulated over the years melted away like ice. But what was truly exciting was that I started to see my body in a different light. I caressed it without embarrassment. I looked at it without embarrassment. I talked about it with courage and without feeling like a pervert.

Along with this feeling came a sense of pride. For the first time in my life I felt that I was capable of fulfilling and satisfying a woman to an extent that raised her to cloud nine, as Marie-Claire said. For the first time, too, I heard a woman speak to me so clearly and say such things. Before that I had suffered from a complex caused by this delicate, thin, fragile body. I didn't expect much from it. It would hurt me to listen to men talking about what they had done to women, and gradually I had become convinced that I was lacking in this regard.

Sometimes I would wonder if this insecurity had something to do with—who knows—the fact that I was the youngest child; or perhaps it had something to do with the illness that had almost taken my life when I was a child; or even that it was divine punishment for what I had done to the stray female donkeys that had gathered in the heat around the well looking for a little water, or the poor ants, scorpions, and birds.

I switched on the light and turned to lie on my stomach. I put her pillow over mine. I crossed my arms and pushed down firmly on the pillow so that the mixture of sweat, perfume, and the odor of a sleeping woman would cling to my pillow. After I did that, I noticed as I contemplated the geometric shapes on the pillowcase, that her head had left a small hollow that could be seen clearly in the light of the bedside lamp. My eyes fell on a strand of hair on the pillow; I then found a second and third. I picked one up. I brought it closer to the lamp.

I examined it for a while before putting it back. After a short while, during which my mind drifted a little, I noticed that the feeling of exhilaration had begun to diminish. I immediately turned off the light. I lay on my back again. I closed my eyes. I started recalling everything that had happened to me with Marie-Claire, stopping at the smallest details, and trying to remember all the emotions reflected on her face. What was strange was that I could hardly believe some of what I recalled because of how amazing it was, although I was certain that it had all actually taken place.

When I woke up, I noticed that daylight had seeped into the room even though the window and curtains were closed. The skies must have been clear, or there were few clouds, I thought to myself. The sun, which was probably hiding behind the buildings, must have risen quite high by then. I glanced at the clock and jumped out of bed. I noticed as I got dressed that the smell of Marie-Claire still clung to my body. I decided not to bathe that day—not because I did not want to or because there was no time, but simply because I wanted to hold on to that smell. I wanted it to stay with me for as long as possible.

Although I was hungry, and the breakfast Marie-Claire had prepared and left on the table for me included much of what I desired, I had only a cup of coffee and a boiled egg. I did so quickly, without bothering to sit down, and then I left the apartment in a hurry.

But instead of going to Belleville where the hotel I worked at was located, I took the metro toward Montparnasse, to where Marie-Claire worked at the post office. I am not sure why I did that. I gave no thought as to whether I had enough time to do so, or of possibly inconveniencing the colleague whom I was to replace, or if the hotel owner, who admired me, might be disappointed if I arrived late. The only thing I felt was a strong internal pull leading me to the Montparnasse post office. It was the first time that had ever happened to me.

In the metro I looked at women with confidence and courage as never before. So, everything is possible with them; with each and every one of them. Yes, I said to myself, everything is possible despite the serious faces and cold, indifferent glances. Even the beautiful ones, who I had thought so difficult that I wondered what male creature could make them open up their bodies, now seemed like all the other women: easy and compliant.

As soon as I got out of the metro station and headed to the post office, I realized that I was about to do something that could put an end to all the beautiful feelings that had engulfed me from the moment I had covered my head with her pillow. Marie-Claire would be very surprised to see me. She would be surprised at my coming to the post office at a time when I was supposed to be at the hotel. It could cause her some discomfort. In fact, she could even be a little frightened because she might think that I was bringing bad news. And what should I tell her when she asked me about my sudden visit? Should I tell her that I was following a mysterious instinct pulling me to her? Or that I wished to know how her face looked that morning? Or that, quite simply, I was not sure how my feet had got me to the Montparnasse post office?

I stopped walking. I sat on one of those wooden benches scattered along the sidewalk to think things over calmly. A few moments later I made a decision that seemed reasonable and practical, and which would somehow abate the powerful force pulling me to her. My plan was to see her from a distance without allowing her to see me; not at the post office, of course, where she would probably be in her office, but on her way to the restaurant where she had her lunch. I knew that she regularly had lunch with her colleagues at that time at a small restaurant near the post office, but there were many small restaurants on both sides of the road, so I decided that I had to focus on the entrance to the post office in order not to miss her as she walked out.

I continued walking as my enthusiasm for this plan increased. When I was a few meters from the post office, I stopped and looked around. I felt lucky when I saw a wide sidewalk with a huge advertising pole near the edge and directly opposite the post office.

I hid behind it and began monitoring the entrance. Moments later I realized that I had put myself in a strange position, because I noticed that some of the passersby must have seen me glued to the pole. They stared at me in confusion and moved away slightly as they might move were they to encounter someone who was crazy, or a strange, homeless person. Feelings of shame and disgust began to sweep over me as I stood there behind the pole, but I did not change my mind, especially as I was certain that it would not be much longer before Marie-Claire came out.

The coming and going in front of the entrance increased and the pace quickened. I neglected no one; I scrutinized everyone entering or leaving. But time passed, and Marie-Claire did not appear. My feelings of disgust and shame grew, and I began to feel anxious. In an effort to overcome all these feelings, I bowed my head a little without taking my eyes off the post office entrance. I began sniffing what still clung to my body of her odor.

None of that worked. In fact I can say with certainty that the effect was quite the opposite of what I had expected. My anxiety increased, and my feelings of shame and disgust did not go away. I also have to add that I noticed as I quickly glanced around me that passersby were looking at me with even greater confusion; what else could they do, I asked myself, when they see a man standing behind an advertising pole staring at a distant point and sniffing himself like a terrified animal?

The minutes went by quickly. It was past one o'clock by then, but there was nothing new at the entrance of the post office except that the foot traffic had slowed down. It seemed that I would not see her after all, even from a distance. She must have had her lunch very early, or maybe she postponed it by an hour or two for some reason, but I could not wait any longer. I had to go to work at once.

9

N
othing stays the same.

That is why we were not really surprised when we went after a while to visit the café where we had first met and found it completely changed. Almost everything about it was different. The counter, the tables and the chairs, the waiters; even the mirrors in which I had first caught sight of Marie-Claire's face were gone. This made the café seem less spacious and less cozy because of all the bare walls.

I was not keen on going to any café that evening. I wanted to go straight home. But Marie-Claire called me so many times that the owner of the hotel, who sat next to me at the reception desk, asked me in his usual kindly manner if there was anything wrong, and if he could help in any way. In the end I agreed, not because she managed to convince me of the pleasure of meeting over a pint of beer as she said, but because I felt that she truly needed to meet and sit at a café before going home. I felt that her need to be in a lively place full of people that evening was beyond her control, even though it was only three days since we'd last been to a restaurant and watched a movie. When I asked her where she would like to meet she replied without a moment's hesitation, "The place where you saw me for the first time."

Marie-Claire, who was waiting for me at the café entrance, insisted that we sit at a table in the same place where we had first exchanged glances. I noticed that she was wearing eyeliner and some light lipstick, which would not have caught my attention had I not been looking at it so intently. I also noticed that she was not depressed, distracted, or annoyed as I had imagined when I had heard her voice on the telephone.

"Why did she insist on meeting me away from home then?" I asked myself, trying to remain calm. As I was searching for an explanation for this need of hers, she stared at me as though reading my mind, and said as she smiled, "It is obvious that you have forgotten this time, too."

"What?"

"What? Your birthday, tomorrow, a few hours from now."

I was a little irritated, but I remained quiet and calm. I was afraid of saying or doing anything that would upset Marie-Claire or spoil her joy at my birthday. It had not occurred to me at all, when she spoke to me over the phone, that she was setting a tight trap for me. Had I known, I would have refused her request; why all this fuss to meet at a café anyway? Could she not have reminded me of this occasion at home?

To tell the truth, I did not need to be reminded; I had not forgotten my birthday, but up to that moment I had gone about my life as if that fact did not concern me, mainly because I was not even sure that I had actually been born on that day. I tried to convince myself many times that I had been, but I never succeeded. Even had I been certain that I had come into this world on the day recorded on my birth certificate, I would have been no more eager to celebrate it. I hate birthdays and find them depressing, contrary to what I am supposed to feel. Life is interrupted on birthdays, energies run low, time seems slow and boring, and you find yourself pretending to be happy for the sake of others. I never truly understood why people should celebrate an event for which they were not responsible, and which they had not chosen, and which brought them closer each year to their death.

I controlled my feelings of irritation and regained my calm. It was clear that Marie-Claire was using the occasion of my birthday to be happy, to celebrate and enjoy life once more. "It is her right to do so," I said to myself. I must hide my innermost feelings from her. I should not tell her what I was thinking. It would not be polite to spoil things for her on this occasion, which seemed to be very important to her.

Marie-Claire did not order beer as she had said she would on the telephone: she ordered hot chocolate. She held the large cup with both hands and raised it slowly to her mouth. She puckered her lips so that the lipstick seemed more obvious. She blew softly on the hot chocolate before taking a small sip. She smacked her lips for a long while after she had put her cup back on the table.

Her left hand remained on the cup handle as usual. After a while, she slid her body with the chair toward me and put her hand between my thighs, transferring some of its warmth to me. I recalled the day when I had stationed myself in front of the post office so that I could watch her from a distance. It occurred to me to tell her that story in all its detail, but I did not, even though I was sure that this was the perfect opportunity to get rid of all these little secrets.

"We must celebrate your birthday and we will start this evening," Marie-Claire said. I nodded in agreement. Removing her hand to take another sip of the hot chocolate and relishing it in a way that inflamed my desire for her, she said, "We will have dinner at a restaurant."

I was not surprised by what she said because I was sure that the celebration would not be complete without a "real outing," as Marie-Claire would say, and the itinerary had to involve dinner at a restaurant, of course.

After we left the café, we took a stroll down the sidewalk along the Luxembourg Gardens fence. Marie-Claire clung to me and took my arm; every once in a while she would lean over and put her head on my shoulder, and my embarrassment would grow whenever anyone passed by. I had to admit that the way she clung to me, kissed and caressed me, and all those little things that Marie-Claire did spontaneously continued to embarrass and disturb me when she did them in public places, even though I knew that hardly anyone paid any attention.

We left the park behind and headed toward the city. She was the one taking the lead. I did not want to interfere. My body was responding obediently to her movements. How nice it was, I thought to myself, for a man to surrender himself to a woman like Marie-Claire; to let her guide him wherever she pleased with her female sensitivity, and her primal intuition and intelligence, neither knowing, nor wishing to know, where she was leading him.

We moved from one sidewalk to another, from one street to another, in silence. I turned to look at her; she smiled. Gradually I forgot my feelings of embarrassment, and feelings of security and some pride replaced my earlier feelings of anxiety. I realized that the celebratory mood was starting to infect me, and that the joy that was becoming increasingly obvious in her glittering eyes was invading me.

"The restaurant we are going to is a surprise," Marie-Claire said in almost a whisper, before she let go of my arm and moved slightly away.

"Don't worry, we're almost there," she added after a little while, as if encouraging me to keep walking. I was not tired, although we had walked a great distance. It did not matter that the restaurant to which she was taking me was far away. For in that wonderful state she was able to transport me to, I was ready to follow her to the furthest restaurant in the city— even if I was exhausted.

Most of the streets we passed by at that time of day were crowded: the cafés were getting ever busier, as usual, and the restaurants were starting to fill up with visitors. All around us was the smell of tobacco, beer, wine, and food; voices and laughter; smiles on lips; eyes full of desire; and, in the fully lit atmosphere, the whiff of sex.

When we arrived at the end of a long road, she stopped in front of a small restaurant. I would not have noticed it had she not pointed it out with her hand. It was situated between two large restaurants. A smiling man stood at its entrance to welcome visitors, and to entice passersby to enter.

"This is the restaurant; we will have French food this evening."

I approached the glass door. I leaned on it to take a peek inside. The small tables were almost touching. The lights were low. The few visitors, who seemed to be tourists, sat away from each other. Some were busy eating, while others just sat looking around.

"I will foot the bill this time," said Marie-Claire as she moved her head closer to the menu hanging near the door. I came closer to her, so she took my arm again and asked, "What do you want to eat on your birthday? How about quail in grapes or ducks in orange? Or maybe you would prefer turkey in wine?'

She named several dishes before bursting out laughing because she knew that I found the names of some French dishes rather silly, even strange. What was the relationship, for example, between a bird such as quail and grapes, which meant you could find them perched together on your plate?

Marie-Claire opened the door and entered, pulling me by my arm. I followed her in as I imagined a featherless turkey, inebriated from drinking too much wine, tossing around in the bottom of a boiling pot.

10

Marie-Claire kept staring at me, and once we had finished our meal, her stares became more obvious and flirtatious.

The state of drunkenness that I was in did not dampen my intuition, which told me that she was preparing for another surprise. The longer she stared at me the more I was convinced that the surprise would be bigger than that of the restaurant. I had never known Marie-Claire to smile like that without good reason.

My intuition proved correct. We had barely taken a few steps from the restaurant when she said, as if unable to contain a secret any longer, "I will take you somewhere that would never have occurred to you."

"What place?"

"Come. Follow me and be quiet."

I said nothing. I followed her submissively. It was her night, I said to myself. It was my birthday, but it was her celebration. After we had walked some distance, I noticed that she was leading me toward the Luxembourg Gardens, and that we were going back through the very streets we had walked on our way to the restaurant. The cafés were busier and louder by then, the restaurants bursting with visitors. The voices and the laughter, the smell of beer, wine, and tobacco, the kisses, glances, and body language, all exuded a head-on celebration of life, in all its smallest pleasures: a loud pagan celebration that awakened all the senses and turned men and women into fragile, insatiable creatures who were curious about and alert to everything happening around them.

Marie-Claire slowed down. She looked at the cafés and restaurants. She stopped before shop windows drenched in light even though the shops were closed. We read out loud some of the advertising posters, and she commented on the images. She did so with great, evident pleasure. Usually I would start complaining after a while, urging her to keep walking, because stopping in front of shop windows drained me and occasionally spoiled my mood. But I followed her silently this time, like an obedient child. I even made an effort to smile at her from time to time so that she could be sure that her slow, disruptive pace did not irritate me.

Marie-Claire took my hand and squeezed it. She caressed my fingers in a way that implied that the contagious celebratory atmosphere was starting to affect her. She encircled my waist with both her arms. She leaned over and clung to me. I felt her breast in my side. I wondered, as I watched her move her head in all directions as though she were looking for something, if the surprise she had for me was one of those crowded cafés, one that was so sweet and special that it would be the crowning event of "our outing" that night.

As I submitted with pleasure to the urge to look at everything around us, to watch everything happening around us, and to catch whatever sounds and scents clung to the breeze and floated around us, I sensed that the contagious celebratory feeling was infecting me, too. I became enveloped by a feeling of profound pleasure, which deepened my state of drunkenness. The weather was warm. The breeze was just damp enough to feel fresh. I felt as if I were ridding myself of all the lethargy and sluggishness caused by the alcohol, and that I was becoming lighter and stronger, and feeling more coherent.

Once we got away from the crowded streets, we continued walking toward the Luxembourg Gardens. Marie-Claire was no longer clinging to me and her arms were no longer around my waist, but she still held my hand. She also stopped looking at shop windows. Our pace picked up once again. We walked along the park fence for a while. It seemed higher and larger at that time of night, when the area around it was so bare. I looked at the huge trees engulfed in the darkness, which turned them into a great black compact mass, their sharp, pointed tops occasionally swaying slowly like boat sails. The breeze grew colder, and the silence began to take hold of the city and became heavier and graver as we moved away from the crowded streets.

I turned to Marie-Claire as we entered an area enveloped by darkness. We continued walking at the same pace on the edge of the sidewalk, very close to the fence and as far as possible from the lights of the street lamps. I could not see the details of her face. I squeezed her hand, and in return she caressed my fingers and stuck closer to me. As I listened to the sound of her heels on the sidewalk I felt that she was ecstatic and as light as air, and that she was living one of those moments during which she was very close to me. I had a strong urge to talk to her, to say something so that I could hear her voice; but I remained silent.

We crossed to the opposite sidewalk after leaving behind the thick darkness. We passed by the café where we had sat a few hours earlier. It was closed, but not all the lights were out because some of the waiters were busy cleaning and rearranging the chairs and tables, causing a racket that could be heard from outside.

We turned and walked toward the Pantheon. I realized at that moment that we were getting closer to where Marie-Claire used to live. The streets were almost empty. There were few cars and even fewer passersby. All the shops were closed. The cafés and restaurants were few. "But where is she taking me?" I wondered as I looked around. For the first time I felt cold, and in search of some warmth; I leaned over her head and encircled her chest with my arm.

We left the Pantheon behind and entered a very narrow street with a sidewalk barely wide enough for one person. I walked a few steps behind Marie-Claire, trying to keep my arms around her chest. I stumbled and our feet became entangled, so I moved away from her. I left the sidewalk to her and I walked on the road, which was not paved but cobbled with small stones that glistened under the street lamps.

"Be careful, the cobbles are smooth; watch your step so that you don't slip."

Moments later she added, as she looked toward the building entrances and their old, large wooden doors, "I like this street; it reminds me of a street in Minelle Menton."

At that moment I felt a great desire to know what it was she wanted to show me; for it seemed to me that the place to which she was taking me was very far, and I was getting colder, especially with the effect of the alcohol wearing off. But I remained quiet. All of a sudden I realized, as I looked at the shop signs, that I had already passed through this street; but when? I was not sure. All I remembered was that I had been alone and the street had not been as empty as it was now.

"Look, there, a star!" she said enthusiastically, pointing to the sky. "Look! There's a second and a third. It's been a long time since I saw stars."

I looked to where she pointed. The three stars were close together and they were very clear; they shone amid seemingly motionless clouds. I became aware that I, too, had not seen stars for a long time. I looked at them for a while then continued walking. The street gradually got steeper so that walking on the cobblestones became more dangerous. I stepped back onto the sidewalk and walked ahead of Mare-Claire this time, leaving about a stride between us so that our feet would not collide. There was no one in the street besides us. There was no movement or sound save that of our foot-steps getting faster as the street got steeper, and the barely audible roar of distant cars.

"Look! Your friends!" Marie-Claire said suddenly as she pointed in the direction toward which we were walking.

"Did you see them?"

I looked to where she was pointing. I saw four home-less people, one of whom was a woman. They had two dogs. They were slowly passing through the street that intersected with the one we were taking. I watched them until they all disappeared. Marie-Claire jokingly called them my friends because she noticed that I cared about them and that I liked to give them a few coins every now and then, ever since I had discovered that they were usually friendly, polite, and pleas-ant, contrary to what their appearance might imply.

When we reached the intersection, we suddenly heard a great commotion accompanied by barking and laughter com-ing from behind us. I turned around immediately, only to see a homeless man walking toward Marie-Claire with open arms as one about to embrace a friend he has not seen in years.

"Come, my little one, come, oh beautiful one."

I was a little frightened and I lunged toward him, but Marie-Claire held my hand and pulled me to her.

"Don't bother."

She was not upset and was unsurprised by his appearance, as if she were expecting him. She laughed and moved her head back so that he could not touch her hair.

"Come, I will love you as no one has ever loved you before."

Marie-Claire clung to me as she went on laughing.

"Come, I will be the most beautiful man in your life."

Marie-Claire pulled me to her again; afraid I would commit some kind of stupidity, and said, "Don't bother. Let him say whatever he wants, he'll go away in a while."

"Come, oh princess."

We continued walking. The laughter of the homeless people behind us got louder again, and the barking intensified. The homeless man followed us for a couple of meters, then turned back to his companions, saying, "I know; I have no luck today. I have no luck today, I know."

"See, no one wants you except me," said a woman with a hoarse voice.

"Who wants this filth?" asked another homeless person.

"He really stinks; he probably hasn't bathed in months."

"Her nose is blocked, but it is better for her that it remains blocked," said another.

Peals of laughter rang out again. Marie-Claire laughed and asked me if I could hear what they were saying. I nodded as I glanced at her handbag, which I suddenly remembered. I stuffed my hands in my pockets. I felt for my official papers, my wallet, my keys. Everything was in its place. I was sure that the homeless there rarely stole. They begged for money, cigarettes, food coupons at restaurants, and sometimes for metro tickets, but they did not rob passersby. Even so, I could not help but feel my pockets just to make sure that everything was fine, especially as I still carried my official papers on me—a long-standing habit that had been aggravated since I had come to live in that city.

"He must have had too much to drink; this is the first time a homeless man has fallen in love with me."

Marie-Claire turned to look behind her as if to make sure that they could not hear what she was saying. She continued in a louder voice, "You know, in Minelle Menton there was an amazing homeless man. Everyone on the street liked him. I think he was the cleanest homeless man I had ever seen in my life. I would only see him in the mornings when I went to school. He would always stand in the same place, and when given a few coins, would raise his hat—he always wore a black hat—and wish you a good day. He always wore clean clothes, sometimes even nice ones, and I could never understand why a man like him had become homeless. Then suddenly he disappeared, and no one knew what happened to him. He was about forty years old. He was not handsome, but he was attractive. Strange, I see him very clearly now; I also remember the sound of his voice and his hand as he moved it to raise his hat."

We parted once more; I left the sidewalk to her as it got narrower and narrower after we crossed the street that intersected ours. I went back to walking on the road but staying close to her because I was sure that she had not yet finished her story about the homeless man.

"Do you think he died?"

"I don't know."

"I tend to think that he did."

"Maybe."

"You know, the homeless die easily here."

"Why?'

"I don't know, but they die easily."

Marie-Claire went quiet for a long moment. I assumed she had nothing more to add about the homeless man or that she didn't want to say anything else. I looked at the sky, searching for the three stars, but saw nothing. No doubt the clouds that had seemed motionless earlier were now hiding the stars from view. "Who knows?" I said to myself. "Maybe they can see them very clearly now in Tunisia, particularly in

Makhaleef village and all its surrounding neighborhoods. Maybe they are shining there now as they shone here a while ago."

I felt cold again. I wrapped my arms around my chest and stroked myself with my fingers, and as I tried to imagine the place to which she was taking me, I was surprised by Marie-Claire pointing to a low door to her right and saying, "Here we are."

I looked at the huge black man standing in front of the door like a statue, and I realized immediately that we were opposite a disco, nightclub, or something of the sort. It was truly a surprise, for this place would not have occurred to me at all. I never thought that Marie-Claire would ever set foot in such a place. I also did not imagine that she would lead me to a disco. And when? On the day that she insists is my birthday.

How did she come up with this strange idea? How could she have allowed herself to lead me from one street to another, and travel all that distance only to bring me to this place? Was it the alcohol that gave her the courage to do so? Was she using the occasion of my birthday to impose her will on me? And did she ask herself whether or not I liked such places?

These questions bombarded me, and I almost lost my temper and shouted in her face, regardless of what the black man, who continued staring at us from the moment we stopped in front of the door, might think. I was overcome by an urge to shout that I hated amusement parks, discos, nightclubs, cabarets, and all those kinds of places. But I remained silent. This time, too, I managed to remain in control of my feelings.

As I focused on the low door, which suddenly opened up to allow two embracing men to come out, Marie-Claire clung to me, saying, "You didn't think I'd bring you to such a place, did you?"

I nodded in agreement. I noticed as I looked at the two young men that one of them was moving his backside to make it appear more prominent.

"What do you think?"

I was lost for words. I just motioned with my head as my eyes followed the two young men, who were walking up the street slowly, turning around to look at me every now and then, and drawing the attention of Marie-Claire, who began to smile.

"Shall we go in?"

"As you wish."

"Let us go in then."

She headed to the door and I followed. The black man gave us a wide smile, which gave me some comfort. He moved back to let us pass through. He knocked on the door, which opened immediately. It was the first time I had ever entered a nightclub. I stumbled and almost fell as I walked over the raised doorsill. She held on to my arm and laughed.

"Be careful, we're going down now. There are three steps."

We walked through a long and narrow path. Marie-Claire was two steps ahead of me. From time to time she laughed and danced to the rhythm of the music, which became louder and clearer as we moved forward. She shook my shoulders and moved them to make me dance like her, and she continued to laugh. Even though I found her laughter strange and somewhat hysterical at that time of night and in that long hallway, which reminded me of a maze, I also started to laugh as I tried to escape from her.

At the end of the hallway was a door I had not noticed because it was painted the same color as the hallway. Marie-Claire pushed it open, and we found ourselves inside the nightclub, only a few meters from a large dance floor filled with a great number of men and women moving like ghosts amid colored lights, which flashed on and off to the beat of loud music.

We spent the rest of the evening there. We danced a lot. Actually, it was Marie-Claire who danced. I was satisfied with moving my arms and feet any which way during the few times that I got up to the dance floor. That night I discovered many things that I had not known about Marie-Claire. I discovered that she loved to dance. I also discovered that she was not as good a dancer as others I saw that night. But the most important discovery was that Marie-Claire danced in a very sexy way. It aroused not only me but others, too, for I noticed that many men were watching her dance with lust-filled eyes.

11

The skies were very clear during the moments that preceded dawn. We walked down what was left of the street where the nightclubs were. We then headed toward the nearest square in search of a taxi. I walked ahead with great strides, ignoring any danger of slipping. From time to time Marie-Claire would catch up with me. She put her hand on my shoulder. She touched my hand. She begged me to slow down and to be careful where I stepped, to avoid slipping. She asked me if I was cold, too. She asked me to wait up for her. But I remained silent, to express my anger, which had grown inexplicably since we had left the nightclub. After a few attempts at drawing a response from me, Marie-Claire also fell silent. What was strange was that her silence made me angrier, as it seemed to me, in my state of excitement, agitation, and fatigue, that her silence shunned and ignored my feelings.

We stood apart in the middle of the empty square and waited. I looked up. The three stars were shining now that the clouds had moved away. I gazed at them for a long time in order to forget, to overcome the feelings that had overtaken me, or at least to reduce their intensity, but it was in vain. My memory refused to give in. Once again I could see Marie-Claire twisting on the dance floor, moving her body in an exciting way. I can see her looking at the man moving closer to her, turning her back to him, moving her lower body as if encouraging him to look at her. I see her spread her legs and feel her breasts and move backward as though she were a stripper. Then there's that mysterious, sexy smile on her lips; those constantly parted lips; that obvious desire in her eyes.

But all these feelings of anger, despite their strength, could not dispel the idea that in reality there was nothing I could blame Marie-Claire for. After all, she had done nothing wrong; all she had done was dance. And because she loved to dance, she did so with enthusiasm, joy, and passion. I am sure that it did not occur to her at all that she danced in a way that excited the men around her.

And now, as I thought of it again, I was even more convinced that her behavior on the dance floor had been spontaneous. What was so strange, I said to myself, about her smiling, closing her eyes, or even shaking her backside in a way that attracted attention? Isn't that all just an honest and spontaneous expression of her joy at dancing? How was it her fault that men looked at her with eyes full of desire? And in any case, most of the women in the nightclub danced in the same way. Some of them were almost nude, which made them even more desirable.

All that was logical and very clear in my mind, but how could I extinguish the fire in my chest? How could I silence the voice inside me that screamed for revenge? How could I put an end to the feeling of anger that overwhelmed and bewildered me?

I knew that I would not be free of any of this unless I said something to annoy her, even if for just a moment. The best way to rid myself of this burden was to blame her, to reproach her, to criticize her. But for what? What could I say to her? I was sure that her reaction would be violent, and that it might mark the beginning of a fight more belligerent than any of our previous fights. Marie-Claire hated comments that referred to her behavior, especially on rare occasions such as this. She liked to live them without barriers and restrictions, to give in to them with as much joy as possible and to gain as much pleasure as possible. She considered any comment on her behavior a rude infringement on her personal life, which she protected fiercely, and a limitation on her freedom, which was something she did not accept, even from the man she loved and lived with under the same roof.

I also feared that she would accuse me of being obsessively jealous and that she would suggest I see a psychiatrist, not only because it hurt whenever she accused me of that, but also because I was afraid that my anger would grow to the point that I would completely lose control and say or do something to her which I would later greatly regret.

"Shut-up then, Mahfouth," I said to myself. "Shut-up well and good. Wait until the storm inside you subsides. Try to use your old tricks, as you did in the early years when the morning breakfast went on forever. Concentrate on one incident and try to delve into it. Recall, if you like, the day your mother died, or slowly read verses of vagrant poetry. You are like them in the end; they were lost in the wastelands and the wilderness, and you are now lost in this city, which is more like a maze. If none of that works, stare at your shoes just as you sometimes stared at the shoes of others in an attempt to identify their personality from their style; or dig into your pockets and look for some crumbs of the Tunisian cake you hid in your pocket when you bought it from the sweet shop in Bellville, exactly as you used to hide the cooked fava beans so that your father would not hurt you.

"And don't forget that today is your birthday and that you are celebrating it, even if you are not too excited about that. It no longer matters whether you were born on this day or not. Forget this confusing point right now; go on as if the date written in the birth certificate is correct. As for your dark ideas about finding birthdays depressing and bringing people closer to death, just stay clear of them.

"Who knows! Maybe you were born with the dawn of such a day or with the final hours of such a night. Maybe you were born at this precise time, and why not? During these very minutes, these very seconds. Now you start your exciting journey, the path ahead gets wider and wider. Your warm body slides and bumps in the darkness into soft, lean, hot walls. The path tightens suddenly; you rest a while and then you push forward with your whole body. You do that several times. You feel that something opens up and out you come.

"Your mother cries with joy. She thinks, as she caresses your small penis as if to make sure you are a boy, that this time she will do the impossible to save you. She will not allow death to come near you. She will not allow it to do to you what it has done to all your siblings who came into this world before you. She will defend you however she can. She will protect you from all dangers. She will not surrender you to fate so quickly this time. She will do her best to save you from death. You must live. You must grow as others grow. For you, she will walk to the end of the earth; she will meet all the witches, soothsayers, saints, tribal wise men, herbalists, and homeopathists.

"You did not die, like all your siblings, but she did. Sometimes you think that she died instead of you. One of you had to die in order for the other to live. One of you had to go so that the other could stay, as if there were only one life for the two of you and it was not possible to share it. It was either you or she . . . and she left. She did not see you all grown up. Her only wish was to see you as tall as the trunk of the cherry tree in front of the house, as she used to say. But death did not grant her the time to do so."

I turned around slightly; I sneaked a look at Marie-Claire. She seemed withdrawn and tired as she stood with her back against an advertising pole, her arms crossed and her head somewhat bowed. I thought that she would not get enough sleep that night, that she had to go to work the next day, and that she must get up early. Instead of feeling vengeful and vindicated, I felt a little sorry for her.

I did not notice her as she moved further and further away from me. She must have done so when I was engrossed in thought. I approached her but she did not move. I moved closer still. I focused on her bowed head, but she remained still and quiet. Could it be that she had fallen asleep while leaning against the pole? I wanted to say something to her, but I could not find anything to say, even though I felt that my anger had dissipated greatly, and that I was regaining my calm. I also felt that I was unable to get any closer to her than I already had. I stamped my heel into the ground. But she did not move. I did it again and again. The fourth time she slowly raised her head and looked at me as though begging me to stop. She lowered her head again and went back to her state of introversion.

Her serene, submissive glance gave me a sense of comfort. I realized, as I recalled my behavior since we had left the nightclub, that the urge within to criticize her had diminished, perhaps because I had achieved an important part of what I had set out to do without becoming embroiled in a fight or uttering harsh words that I might later regret. Weren't my unusual silence, my ignoring her questions, and the fact that I paid her no heed at all, other ways of criticizing her after all, I wondered?

I heard the roar of a car engine. I stiffened at the edge of the sidewalk as soon as I was certain that it was a taxi and that the light on its dashboard meant it was available. I raised my hand high and waved it about; I was worried that the driver would not see me. The car, which continued down the road at the same speed, suddenly stopped, causing its wheels to screech loudly in the dead of night. As I opened the back door for Marie-Claire, the driver—who appeared, from what I could see of his features, to be an Arab—asked me where we were heading. When I told him, he ordered me to shut the door and look for another taxi because he was on his way home and would only take passengers who lived somewhere along his route.

The car took off at a crazy speed. I felt as I watched it drive away that what had just happened provided a good opportunity to get closer to Marie-Claire, who had resumed her position against the advertising pole, and in particular, to break the barrier of silence between us. I expressed my annoyance at the driver to her. She turned to me and smiled. That encouraged me to say more. I told her that taxi drivers were the same everywhere and that they were scum. She burst out laughing. My enthusiasm increased, and I added loudly that they were fuckers and sons of bitches, too. She looked at me in admiration and took my arm, laughing all the while. I felt even more encouraged and went on swearing in Arabic at taxi drivers in every city in the world as Marie-Claire's giggles turned into roars of laughter.

12

tried not to make a sound as I opened the door. The room was dark, but there was a faint light entering from the street through the curtains, which were not completely closed, and which also allowed me to see the bed clearly. I approached it slowly. I removed the cover and slid into bed.

As soon as my head hit the pillow, I realized that I was wearier than I had thought, and that the day, which would be over after a few endless minutes, seemed very long. Unlike other days, my work at the hotel had worn me out. And the lecture that I was to give to the students tomorrow, after a long absence from teaching, had taken longer to prepare than I had expected.

Marie-Claire was lying on her right side facing the window. I listened for her breathing and deduced from its evenness that she was fast asleep. I lay on my back and began thinking of what I had just read as I waited to join her. Suddenly I felt her move and turn to face me. I felt her hand fall heavily on the top of my shoulder; I heard her mumble:

"What was your relationship with her like?"

I did not say anything and I did not move. I thought she was dreaming. But I was surprised by her warm fingers sliding over my shoulder, and I heard her ask the same question again, this time with a clearer voice.

"What was your relationship with her like?"

"Whom are you talking about?"

She fell silent for a while as though afraid to reply.

"Your mother."

"My mother? What made you think of her now?"

"I don't know."

I no longer remembered when I had first spoken to Marie-Claire about my mother. I also do not know why I had once told her that what remained in my memory of her facial features had begun to fade, and that I could not recall those features from photographs, as my mother had never stood in front of a camera. But ever since I had told her all that, my mother had became a topic that Marie-Claire enjoyed talking about.

It was obvious from the many questions she heaped on me that what she felt for my mother was part compassion and even part affection. I cannot deny that I sometimes admired her as I listened attentively to what she had to say, and it seemed to me that she paid far greater attention to my mother than to her own, who was forgotten in some rural village.

Sometimes I was annoyed by all this attention, however, because I felt that Marie-Claire was subconsciously turning my mother into an exotic, attention-grabbing topic, an interesting, curious one that satisfied her curiosity, enriched her imagination, and fed her inquisitive nature.

Here she was returning to the subject again, and because I was certain she would not stop asking her questions until I had answered her, I said in a very low voice so that she could understand that I was very tired, "It was an ordinary relationship. I loved her and she loved me."

And to put an end to the subject quickly, I added, making use of her silence, "That's all there is to it, and anyway, you know that; I already told you. Now I must sleep, and you, too, must sleep."

I waited a little to make sure she was convinced of what I had said. She remained silent. But the moment I turned my back to her she spoke again, "I don't understand . . . how can you bear her face fading away?

I sought an answer with which to end the conversation.

Marie-Claire added, "I can't . . . just the thought of it torments me."

"She is in my heart, and she will always be there. That is what is important."

"Do you look like her?"

"Yes, a lot; that's what everyone tells me."

"Do you remember the color of her eyes?"

"Yes, she had the same color eyes as mine—deep green."

"And was she tall like you?"

"No, the height I inherited from my father."

I remembered at that moment that I was the only child in the neighborhood to have green eyes, and because of that they used to call me the albino. It hurt a lot, and I sometimes cried when I was alone, and I used to secretly curse God for not creating me with black eyes like everyone else.

As I thought of telling that to Marie-Claire, to stop her from talking about my mother, I heard her say, "I like the story of the lock that your mother buried."

I was slightly annoyed, but I was determined to remain calm in order not to complicate things.

"How did you feel when you heard that story for the first time?"

"I don't remember any more. You know, some people don't believe the story and think it's just superstition."

"Superstition? A story like that can't be superstition, but there's something I don't understand. Why did she bury the lock near the house? Why didn't she bury it far away?"

"I don't know. It is said that she buried it there, but no one knows for sure."

"And you didn't ask your mother about it?"

"Never."

"Strange!"

"I was too young for these things."

"And she never spoke to you about it?"

"Never. She never spoke to me about the lock or the place where she buried it."

"Maybe because she didn't know you knew."

"Maybe."

"Or maybe it was also because the old people who advised her asked her not to tell you anything."

I said nothing. Marie-Claire drew closer to me. She began moving her fingers very slowly over my lower back. Usually I would turn around and take her in my arms, but this time I remained motionless.

"And your father, didn't he tell you anything about the lock?"

"He said nothing."

She clung tightly to me so that I could feel her breasts touching my upper back; she then put one of her legs between my thighs as she continued to caress me with her fingers.

"If I were in your place I would have asked her where she'd buried the lock."

I realized at that moment that everything I had done to make her be quiet had been in vain. As I dragged myself to the edge of the bed to disentangle myself, I said loudly, "Can't you understand? I want to sleep. I want to sleep."

Contrary to what I had expected, Marie-Claire did not react. In fact she seemed kind and gentle.

"Don't get angry, I just wanted to express my admiration for your mother."

Before turning her back to me, to indicate that she was about to stop talking completely, she added, "If it were not for her, you would have died years ago!"

Her last sentence stayed in my mind for a long time. From time to time I managed to drive it away, but it soon returned.

I could not go to sleep. After tossing and turning in bed for a while, I buried my head in my pillow, determined not to move and not to open my eyes. When I raised my head to look around me I noticed that the room was not as dark as before. I did not know how long I had slept, but I knew was that it had been a dream-filled sleep.

I saw myself on a train. I was not alone. My mother was sitting next to me. She was happy, not because she was with me, but because she was taking the train for the first time. When she turned to me, I gazed at her face and its most intricate details. "It is as if you are seeing me for the first time," my mother said, smiling. I kept scrutinizing her face without saying a word. I noticed that she was a little different from the mother I had known before her features faded from my memory, but this did not bother me, as I was certain that the woman sitting next to me was my mother.

"What is that?" she asked as she pointed outside.

"Sunflowers."

"Sunflowers?"

"Yes."

"What do they do with them?"

"They extract oil from them."

"Oil?"

"Yes."

"A different kind of oil, with a different taste. Not like olive oil."

I moved to the vacant seat opposite her. She moved her head slowly to see the fields of sunflowers extending to the horizon. Her eyes were wide open, full of admiration for what she was seeing.

"How yellow they are. It is as if we are in a dream," she said in a whisper.

I felt a strong urge to ask her if she had gone to heaven, but I did not dare. A peculiar form of embarrassment prevented me from posing the question. I noticed at that moment that she did not ask me about everything that had happened to me since her death. I thought of telling her that it was a good thing that she had listened to the village elders and buried the lock, and that were it not for her I would have died a long time ago, but I decided against that, because I believed that delving into these topics might remind her of old sadnesses and spoil the feeling of happiness that enveloped her at that moment.

The train stopped at a small station. There was no one on the platform except Marie-Claire and her mother, Madame Sar. They greeted us with great warmth and insisted on carrying our luggage to where the car was waiting to take us to her mother's house, which was located outside the village. All the way Marie-Claire kept her eyes on my mother who sat next to her in the back seat.

As soon as we entered the house and sat down in the living room, Marie-Claire's mother said, "Your son is the first Arab to enter our house and you are the second."

My mother replied, in colloquial Tunisian, that she was sure that her son had chanced upon some good French people. I realized at that moment that they understood each other even though each was speaking her own language. But I did not find that strange. I also did not find it strange when they called each other by their names even though I did not remember introducing them by name at the station.

"Make yourself at home, Madame Turki. Relax. If you would prefer to sit somewhere else, do not hesitate."

"God bless you, Madame Sar, I am fine where I am. May God give you long life and keep Marie-Claire safe from harm."

A short while later, Marie-Claire and her mother both sat next to my mother on the same long sofa; one to her left, the other to her right. They got closer to her; they gazed at her and smiled.

"How beautiful you look right now, Madame Turki. Your clothes are beautiful and bright. What fabric is this? Silk, linen, or cotton?"

They touched the edges of her peplos style dress and ran their fingers tenderly over the fabric; they then leaned in for a closer look.

"Your necklace is also lovely, Madame Turki, and this ring on your finger and those bracelets! The kohl on your eyes. The tattoo on your forehead. The siwak in your mouth. The henna on your hands. The color of your eyes, your skin, your teeth."

My mother did not stop smiling; she looked at me every now and again, as if calling for my help, as though she wanted me to help her bear all these compliments, which she was apparently not expecting. I smiled back at her, happy that the meeting I had been so apprehensive about was going very well.

Marie-Claire and her mother did not leave their guest alone until they noticed that they had spent a little longer than necessary sitting next to her on the sofa, and that it was time to go to the kitchen to prepare dinner. My mother seized the opportunity to tell me that I was really lucky and that life was smiling at me. In fact, life was spoiling me after the deprivation I had suffered during my childhood, as she had never imagined that I would marry a woman so beautiful and sensible—although she always knew that I would end up with good people. I wanted to tell her that Marie-Claire was not my wife, that I was living with her in sin, and that she was not as sensible as she thought, but I did not.

My mother got up from the sofa. She moved in a leisurely way around the living room. She stopped in front of some furniture. She looked at it intently. She leaned over it, touched it, smelled it. She touched some of the items crowding the mantelpiece, the television stand, and the bookshelves. She examined them. She turned them over very carefully. She asked me what some of them were called.

I resumed my scrutiny of her face so that all its fine details and features would remain clear in my mind for the rest of my life; so that I would not forget them as I had done before. I knew that she would go back from whence she came, and that she would disappear as mysteriously as she had appeared when we surrendered to sleep. I thought, of course, of taking many pictures of her, but I expelled this idea from my mind because I thought it inappropriate to take pictures of the dead. The dead are dead, I said to myself, and invading their secret world in such an uncouth manner hurts and harms this world. I was also afraid that taking photographs of the dead was sinful or prohibited.

When we heard Marie-Claire calling from the kitchen to announce that everything was ready, I started explaining to my mother how she should behave at the dinner table: that she should hold the fork in her left hand, cut the bread with a knife, close her mouth when chewing her food, not talk with her mouth full, remain seated, and get up only if absolutely necessary.

My mother took a piece of round sliced bread spread with a thick layer of foie gras. She took a bite.

"How do you find it?" asked Marie-Claire's mother..

"Very tasty. What is it?"

"It is a pâté made of duck liver. We eat it at Christmas and on other big occasions. We bought it especially for you. Would you like another slice?"

My mother nods.

"Do you know, Madame Turki, it seems your son does not like foie gras," added Marie-Claire, who had been silent until that moment. "He says he gets a stomachache every time he eats it. He also says he likes neither its color nor its taste. He hated it even more when he saw a documentary on television about farmers in the Dordogne region opening the beaks of poor ducks and geese to plunge in a tube with which to force feed them to make them fat and their livers huge."

My mother said nothing, but her occasional glances at me lasted longer and became more intense. When she was finished with the main dish and before we moved on to the cheeses, I remembered something vital that I had forgotten to tell my mother when listing how she should behave at the table. I forgot to tell her that the red liquid that they were drinking with the meal was alcohol. Luckily my mother had only one glass. She confirmed that to me several times, but this single glass was enough to turn my mother into another human being.

"I want you to try this piece of Roquefort, Madame Turki," said Marie-Claire's mother as she leaned over a big plate full of various cheeses. "All these cheeses are from our country." My mother devoured a piece of cheese and presented her plate immediately to Marie-Claire's mother, who was happy to see my mother's unexpected appetite for her cheeses.

"And now, how about a small piece of Pont L'évêque?"

"Delicious," said my mother as she passed her plate back again.

"Have a piece of this Chausée Aux Moix; and this piece of Camembert; and this piece of Brie de Meaux; and this and this . . . ."

I watched the scene in disbelief, but what happened to me next was beyond belief. We finished dessert, which my mother consumed with surprising greed and voracity. Marie-Claire's mother put an open box of chocolates on the table. My mother eyed it with pleasure. Then she suddenly leaned her head and asked me sharply, "Why don't you like foie gras?" I smiled at her, but I remained quiet. But my mother asked me again, this time in a sharper tone. Marie-Claire and her mother stopped moving and a heavy silence ensued. I had no idea what to tell her. "You are now civilized and you refuse even the foie gras from your kind mother-in-law."

"It doesn't matter," said Marie-Claire. "He likes many other things."

"But how can he refuse the foie gras?" shouted my mother.

Marie-Claire's mother intervened to clam her down. "I also dislike many things. Don't worry about it; please."

But my mother did not stop. "It is not polite for a stranger to refuse something that his hosts, who have welcomed him, love. It is not polite to contradict them and to refuse their food," said my mother before bursting into bitter tears. I moved closer to her in an effort to soothe her.

"Stay where you are. I don't want you to touch me. You will lose yourself; you will die if you persist in your stubbornness."

"Please mother, don't cry."

"Don't come near me. Don't touch me. I'm not your mother."

Marie-Claire sat next to her. She took her hand. She attempted to calm her down as she wiped the tears from her cheeks. Marie-Claire's mother got closer and expressed her willingness to do whatever she wanted. But my mother would not stop crying, nor did she stop criticizing me. I tried for a while to find a solution to this problem, and then walked out into the garden.

13

couldn't bear to see my mother crying so bitterly. I also couldn't bear the dream ending in this strange and sudden way. I wished that it could have gone on long enough for my mother to forgive my mistake, to be happy with me once again, to go back to the way she'd been, or at least to stop crying so bitterly.

I was overwhelmed by pain mixed with guilt. I tried convincing myself that everything that had happened to me with my mother, who had died a long time ago, was nothing but a passing dream that I would forget in a couple of days. But I could not. I switched my thoughts to the topic of my lecture the next day. I thought of the significance it would have after a long absence from teaching. I recalled some of what I had prepared and I started reciting some of my favorite verses of vagrant poetry. But the image of my mother crying bitterly and repeating the words, "Do not come near me, do not touch me, I am not your mother," overwhelmed me once again.

I could not stop myself from tossing and turning in bed, and for fear of disturbing Marie-Claire's sleep, I left the bedroom. I stretched out on the sofa in the living room and closed my eyes. I was certain that two more hours of sleep would be enough to help me face the burdens of the day about to dawn. But sleep eluded me again that night. So I got up, washed quickly, dressed quickly, and left the apartment.

The city streets were empty. The sidewalks seemed wider. The weather was not as cold as I had expected. I walked around aimlessly. I took big strides at first, as if trying to escape from the apartment, as if I wanted to move as far and as fast as possible from the place where I had dreamed of my mother crying so bitterly. After walking for quite a distance, I slowed down.

Life began to stir in the streets. Gradually the number of buses increased, as did the number of street cleaners wearing their green uniforms and pushing the dirt everywhere on the streets into the drains opposite with their huge brooms. They talked and laughed out loud. Most of them were Arabs and blacks; some spoke Berber.

For the first time since I had got up that morning, I felt my sensations of pain and guilt receding and that I had finally begun to unburden myself of my dream. That made me happy, and I decided to continue walking to regain my calm before returning to the apartment for breakfast with Marie-Claire. But I realized suddenly that I had walked quite a distance from where I lived, and that it had become impossible for me to return before Marie-Claire went to work, even if I were to run back.

That did not bother me too much. On the contrary, deep down I felt that Marie-Claire deserved to be deprived of the pleasure of breakfast because everything that had happened to me the day before had been her fault. Had she not mentioned my mother and the lock she had buried I would not have had that strange dream. It was not important that I return to the flat. I could keep strolling. I gazed for a long time at the huge locked wooden doors of the buildings. I watched taxis traveling streets at high speeds. I watched, from afar, the few elderly people who were now taking their dogs out to urinate and defecate on the sidewalk. I could smell freshly brewed coffee and freshly baked bread coming from the cafés and the few bakeries that had opened their doors early. When I got tired, or bored with walking, I sat at a café. I slowly sipped some coffee or hot chocolate. I might have had something light to eat because I was not hungry. I then headed to the hotel to work for a couple of hours before going to the university.

I changed direction. After crossing many identical streets, I realized that contrary to what I had thought, I had to go back to the apartment first for my books and the materials I had prepared for the lecture. I guessed, as I looked at the increasing number of students along the sidewalks, that it was way past seven o'clock. Marie-Claire would have woken up by then. I imagined her turning over and reaching out her hand to find no one there. There was no doubt in my mind that she would be gentler and kinder than she had been when she had decided to stop talking completely about my mother the day before. When she opened her eyes she must have thought for some time about what had happened between us before we slept, and realized that her incessant questions about my mother and her lock at that time of night were very annoying.

She would look for me in the kitchen, then in the bathroom, and then in the bathroom. She would call out my name once, twice, or three times to make sure that I was not hiding somewhere in the apartment. As she prepared her breakfast she would notice that I had had nothing to eat. She would also notice that I had forgotten to take my cell phone with me. She would wait for me a little while after watering her plants and setting the table and when she had finally given up on my returning home, she would have her breakfast quickly and leave the flat immediately in order not to be late for the post office.

In the metro she would look at the faces of travelers for a long time. She would also look at those seated on the benches scattered around the station platforms; she would wonder what had made me disappear in this strange way and what she could do to make sure I was fine. It would occur to her to call the owner of the hotel where I worked. But she would decide against that unless I did not return to the flat at the usual time. At the post office she would try to forget all of this. She would lean over the mail trolleys, as she had done during her first days on the job. She would look at the stamps, read the addresses, and smell the letters.

But she would not be able to hide or overcome her anxiety. She would not succeed in appearing calm and normal in front of her colleagues. She would remain distracted and would be unable to contain her nervousness until I returned home in the evening. I imagined her pursing her lips in the way she does when she is upset and nervous, and I smiled. "You deserve this and much more," I said to myself. "In future you must think long and hard before opening your mouth about my mother and her lock."

The pedestrian traffic suddenly increased. It was as if most of the inhabitants of the neighboring building had emerged from their homes the same at time, as though by unspoken agreement. The din and honking of cars, trucks, and buses, no longer able to move fast enough, got louder, and a traffic jam ensued, a din that was interspersed every now and again with the curses of drivers whose patience had worn thin.

To pass the time until the opening of schools and other institutions had swallowed and then lightened the vehicle and pedestrian traffic, and to escape the noise and, particularly, the fumes and gases emitted by old trucks, I quickly entered the first shop along my way. I realized, after a taking a couple of steps inside, that I was in the Galleries La Fayette. I did not notice this at first because I went in by a side entrance rather than the main entrance, which I knew very well.

I was overcome with happiness. I liked supermarkets and large department stores. I only found it comfortable and enjoyable to walk around in them when they were not crowded, of course. For that reason I avoided entering, or even passing them in the run-up to Christmas and the New Year.

I was even happier to find myself in the perfume department, and what they call here, "the soft underwear" department. I admit that these sections in large department stores attracted my attention more than any other. For this reason I always found myself drawn to the Bazaar Hotel de Ville, Les Printemps Department Store, Gallarie Lafayette, and Montparnasse Shopping Center for their large and very elegant perfume and women's underwear departments.

Attractive displays of dozens of pieces of underwear, tiny panties, and bras in many colors, mostly light pink, red, and white. Most of them were designed with soft, transparent fabrics and lace, intended to expose and excite rather than provide modest cover. Dozens of perfume bottles in various sizes, neatly and tastefully arranged on clear glass shelves. Saleswomen, mostly young and pretty, wearing full make-up. Huge mirrors everywhere. Add to this the soft intoxicating feminine atmosphere, the scent of new fabrics mixed with the scent of the saleswomen, and the customers, mostly women, and the free perfume samples. Dear God! What place could be softer and more beautiful than this? What other place could be more soothing to one's nerves and better able to relieve the mind of stressful detractions than this department into which fate had delivered me on that depressing morning?

I took a stroll in the department: a long and slow stroll. I had enough time before I had to get back to the apartment before going to the hotel. Every time I thought of leaving so as not to attract the attention of the security guards, who would start watching me and end up restricting my freedom and spoiling this delightful wander for me, a strong urge compelled me to stay. I roamed from hall to hall, stopping occasionally. I felt the soft clothes. I inhaled the perfume samples. I watched the women inspecting and feeling the underwear and bras. I looked at the beautiful saleswomen and could not believe that they were smiling at me and me alone. And when I left the place, I felt that everything that had bothered me as a result of the dream of the night before had faded away to be replaced by a sensation not unlike exhilaration.

When I got home that evening Marie-Claire was as angry with me as I had expected. I retaliated by blaming her for all that had happened. She shouted at me and criticized me for many things. I remained silent, waiting for her to calm down, but she would not stop shouting; on the contrary, she got angrier and started swearing at me. So I started swearing at her. I called her weak. I said that she suffered from low self-esteem, and most dangerous of all, I called her a coward who went to pieces if she woke up in the morning to find herself alone. I blurted out everything quickly and in a single breath to prevent her from interrupting me.

She stopped shouting and eyed me coldly. It was obvious that she was surprised by the words that had unwittingly escaped my lips. Marie-Claire nodded her head imperceptibly, and her eyes, which remained fixed on me, signaled that she was at the peak of her anger. I felt some regret for what I had said, but I did not apologize for it. I remained firmly in place and returned her gaze until she went to the bedroom and slammed the door so hard the walls shook.

Afterward, and as usual, Marie-Claire resorted to her devastating weapon: silence. I was ready to face the effect of this weapon. I had learned, with time, to tolerate the noticeably torturous and destructive effects it had on the soul. But the problem was that her silence this time lasted longer than necessary. I suffered, and endured a great deal, psychologically and sexually, for this time she decided not to utter a single word to me, and more seriously, not to touch me or let me come close to her in bed or anywhere else.

After much hesitation I admitted to her that I had made a mistake by leaving the apartment unusually early that morning without letting her know what I had planned to do. And I admitted to the other, even more unforgivable mistake of letting her worry about me for a whole day by not calling her as I should have to let her know that I was all right.

Marie-Claire paid my admission no heed; sometimes it seemed as though she used it to withdraw even further from me into her solitude. I did not let despondency get the better of me. I repeated my confession in various ways and at various times, but it was as if I were talking to a brick wall.

Days later I found myself forced to do what I had been avoiding up to that moment: to apologize to her for everything I had done. I apologized even though I was not fully convinced of what I was doing, for Mare-Claire had been responsible for everything that had happened, although I admit to having been somewhat harsh in calling her a coward and accusing her of having no self-confidence.

Marie-Claire remained in her cocoon of displeasure and anxiety, and she remained distant for over two weeks. I did not succeed in making her talk or in bringing her out of her shell until I spoke to her, with forced enthusiasm, about the fast-approaching summer vacation, and especially when I asked her with some insistence about the country she wanted to travel to.

14

I do not think that Marie-Claire loved any word more than she did the word 'vacation.' This word had a magical, wondrous effect on her. When she said it, her eyes sparkled, and her round face gave off a combination of spontaneity and calm, making her seem like a happy little child.

Every year Marie-Claire insisted that we pack our bags and travel. She often said that there could be no holiday without travel. No holiday without adventure, without a delicious tiredness. In the early years, I showed no enthusiasm for traveling unless she agreed to accompany me to Tunisia because I never gave vacations much importance and never believed they deserved so much trouble. To me, a vacation meant taking a break from work and spending the day at home to rest, strolling down the streets, watching a movie, or watching people in parks.

I remember Marie-Claire suggesting, two years after we had met, that we travel to Tanzania to spend a few days in Zanzibar, "the island of spices and coconuts," as she said. I immediately refused, without even asking her where this Zanzibar, located on the shores of Tanzania, was. But Marie-Claire insisted.

"What have I got to do with Tanzania?" I asked her furiously. "Should I travel all this distance to see spices?"

"Aren't you African?" She asked me in surprise. It was the first time in my life that I became acutely aware that I was indeed African.

This time we traveled to Crete, where we spent two whole weeks. As usual, I came back exhausted. Even now, two weeks after our return, I still feel some of that tiredness, which I had never before felt on a vacation.

From the moment we landed on the island of Crete to the moment we left, Marie-Claire did not give me a chance to catch my breath or rest, taking advantage, no doubt, of my earlier criticisms in order that she could forgive me and completely forget what I had said during our last fight. Several times, I was even denied a midday siesta, which I always took in the summer.

"We didn't come here to sleep!" she would say mockingly. "We didn't travel all this way to go to the beach and lie on the sand for hours like foolish tourists whose only concern is to get a tan, or sit at cafés at the port and watch the moored boats"—which was what I had suggested from time to time. "Crete is a big island. There are amazing places and sites we must visit. There are important things we must discover." Throughout our stay she was always ready to move from place to place. I do not recall that she gave in to weariness or complained of anything; and she was now very satisfied with our richly eventful holiday, as she enthusiastically and cheerfully intoned. For this reason, she appeared calm and relaxed, as though she had accomplished an important task. She also treated me with great kindness, responding quickly to my every whim, including those of a sexual nature.

Unlike previous trips, we did not stay at a hotel or even at a room rented from locals—which is what Marie-Claire preferred. She believed that staying at hotels, especially like the ones we occasionally stayed in, spoiled one's enjoyment of a vacation and robbed one of the opportunity to mix with the locals, listen to their conversations, get to know their opinions and thoughts about life, eat their food, and discover their habits and traditions.

We spent the entire holiday camping. That came as no surprise to me, for Marie-Claire had made sure to inform me of this from the moment Crete was chosen as our holiday destination. It was as if she wanted me to be psychologically prepared for such an adventure because she knew that I had never been on a camping holiday before.

The camping site she took me to was a dusty piece of land, except for some parts with a few eucalyptus trees. It was surrounded by a low, gypsum-painted wall. At the entrance there was a wooden hut for the guard. It was very similar to the Makhaleef village square, which was transformed every Thursday into a bustling market for goats, cows, and camels. And what made it appear more deserted was that it was about three kilometers from the town where we decided to stay. "We must move as far away as possible from the cities and their noise," said Marie-Claire as we passed the toilets, washbasins, and shower rooms, which seemed clean from the outside, on our way to the spot assigned to us by the guard to pitch our tent. "We must enjoy the space, the openness, and the silence. There is nothing more beautiful and more comforting to body and soul than sleeping on the ground in the open air, close to the sky and the stars. We must also stay away from crowds of tourists. People here are simple and real, and more importantly, most of them are inhabitants of Crete."

Fortunately there was a tree in the area assigned to us. Marie-Claire immediately pulled out her old tent, which she had used as a student, from one of the bags. She had thought it was lost or that she had thrown it away, but a few days before we were due to travel she discovered that her mother, who hoarded every useless thing, from cardboard boxes and empty champagne bottles to colored wrapping paper, had kept the tent, which Marie-Claire had left with her many years ago.

It did not take long to pitch the tent. We did it easily. In truth, it was Marie-Claire who put it up. I was satisfied with helping her because I had no idea how to erect these things, which differed from the tents of Bedouins and shepherds, with which I was well acquainted.

We then prepared and cleaned the surrounding area. I sprayed water around the tent so that the dust would not be disturbed with our every move, but before that, I had gathered all the stones, sticks, and dead bugs, and thrown them far away. I also used some small twigs to make what resembled a broom and I swept the area well. Marie-Claire opened her small box of medicines, which she always took with her on her travels; she took out the insecticide and sprayed the area immediately surrounding the tent. "Don't worry. You can sleep calmly now," she said, smiling. She pretended to have forgotten to spray an area, so she went back to spray it with exaggerated caution, looking at me all the while to ensure I was watching the whole operation so that I would feel better and stop my incessant talk about insects, and scorpions in particular, of which Marie-Claire knew I had a real phobia.

Darkness was already spreading around us when we finished our work. Everything inside and outside the tent was as good as could be. Before dinner, we took a long walk around the camping area. There were not many campers yet, so the tents were spaced far apart. In front of most of them stood men, women, and children, and next to the tents were bicycles, motorbikes, and cars. As we passed each tent, Marie-Claire turned to the owners and greeted them with a word, a hand gesture, or a nod of her head. "I like camping," she said, as if presenting an excuse for her actions. "People here are not cold and introverted like hotel guests. They smile at you. They greet you. They treat you as if they know you. You will see once the campsite is full, you will feel it with each passing day. You will feel like you are part of a big family."

We did not feel the passage of time, as we were constantly on the move. We had a different program for each day, decided by Marie-Claire, with my approval of course. As soon as we finished dinner—usually canned food, vegetables, and fruits—Marie-Claire would pull her maps from her bag and spread them out on the floor. She would shine her flashlight, which never left her side at night, looking for cities and towns that she would then suggest we visit the next day.

As soon as she had finished doing that, she would open the travel books and guides she was carrying. She would read out loud and with great pleasure, which I could detect in the way she pronounced the words, everything that was written about these villages and towns, emphasizing the differences between one and the other. She would not stop reading until I started yawning, thereby announcing that I would like to sleep. I would slide my body into the sleeping bag and close my eyes, but Marie-Claire would continue looking over her evidence and maps. And, before she entered her own sleeping bag or mine, naked—which is what she did when she yearned for me or felt that I longed for her—she would prepare everything that we might need for the next day. She would take out the clothes that we were to wear, and whatever we needed to carry with us or cover our heads with so that we did not get sunstroke. She would empty her bottle so that it would be ready for refilling in the morning. She would put the medicine box, creams, sunglasses, and the novels and magazines we were reading in the bag that she was going to carry so that she would not forget them, and more specifically, so that we would not waste time looking for everything in the morning.

We would wake up early most days, as transportation between the camping site and the station in the town from which the buses left to the various cities of Crete were infrequent and slow. Sometimes we were forced to walk some of the distance rather than spend time getting bored waiting for transportation.

We visited many villages, towns, and historic and natural sites, where we spent several hours or most of the day. In fact, we visited so many places that I started to confuse their names, especially if they were similar. I do not believe that I have visited as many difference places in my whole life as I did during this short period.

We would return to the camping site late. After dinner, Marie-Claire would go back to scrutinizing her maps and flipping through her travel books. Sometimes I would express my consent to the next day's plan and succeed in shaking her off. I would take the few plates that we had used for our meal and head to the washbasins, for I had noticed that many of the women staying at the camping site, which had filled up, went to the shower rooms at that time.

I would place the dishes in one of the basins from which I had a good view of the women's movement, and so as not to raise the suspicion of the men and women around me, I would pour a lot of washing-up liquid over the dishes and turn on the faucet all the way. Water would gush out, filling the basin with lather. This way I could wash the same dishes over and over, and prolong my stay without anyone noticing that I had only a handful of dishes whose washing did not need all that time. Occasionally I would raise my head to look at the women who were coming out of the shower rooms semi-naked, their wet, warm bodies emitting the scent of perfumed soap.

During the second week of the holiday, and particularly during the last part of the week, I stopped expressing any interest in the daily program. My only concern was to go every evening after dinner to the washbasins. As I expected, Marie-Claire took advantage of this more than I had first expected to plan programs that would never have occurred to me.

One day, after waking me up earlier than usual, she asked me to put on my lightweight sandals because the gorges she told me about yesterday were very dangerous. At that moment I felt some regret at not having asked her about the gorges she intended on taking me to, but I said nothing.

We got on an old bus, which took us to a mountain peak by a winding narrow road, unpaved in many places. Sometimes the bus would lean to the right or left as if about to plunge into the pine forest bordering the road.

The tourists would scream and laugh like children on an exciting and adventurous trip. When the bus crossed the unpaved spots on the road, which got worse and worse as we neared the peak, its wheels would raise a cloud of dust so thick it would obscure our vision and seep into the bus. The tourists would rush to close the windows, but some windows did not shut properly or did not shut at all. They would close their eyes, cover their faces with their hats, wave their hands about in the air, or change their seats to protect themselves from the dust, laughing and screaming all the time, making them seem even more like children. Marie-Claire held my hand and clung to me as she watched the commotion around her like one who had suddenly stumbled upon an exciting scene and did not want to miss a thing.

She was truly happy that day. Not only because I did not object to the idea of crossing that long gorge, which extended from the mountain peak to the sea, but also because I agreed, without any discussion, to wear a pair of shorts and a sleeveless shirt—something I usually refused to do in public, even though I knew that Marie-Claire liked to see me in these clothes sometimes. What usually made me refuse to wear such clothes was the fact that I felt embarrassed and shy about revealing my knees, and especially my hairy and slightly bowed legs.

The gorge was not very different from the rose-colored gorges carved out by the heavy downpours and seasonal floods around Wad al-Kharub in Makhaleef village. I knew those gorges well, as I had crossed them many times as a child. That was why I did not feel the same pleasure as Marie-Claire on that day. The only thing that caught my attention was that it was longer and deeper at some points, particularly the beginning, and that it was less dangerous because over time the thousands of tourists who had walked here before us had left a clear passage between the thorns, plants, and sharp stones.

We crossed it in over three hours, including the many rest stops along the way, of course, which provided Marie-Claire with the opportunity to take many pictures of anything that took her fancy: houses and small abandoned huts; a goat climbing the sides of the gorge looking for pasture; streams where unfamiliar plants grew; large pink rocks; dry mounds, hills, and valleys.

From time to time I would be surprised to find the camera pointing at me, and its zoom lens, which looked like the barrel of a small canon, aimed at me. "Don't move," she would say to me. Every holiday, she would take many pictures of me, most of them in black and white. She loved photography and owned three cameras, but when I suggested I take picture of her, she was not so keen because she did not like photographs of herself, and, besides, found real pleasure in photographing others.

When we reached the sea, and to pass the time as we waited for the remaining members of our group to cross the gorge, we went for a swim as had all those who had got there before us. Then we got onto a boat headed for a small village, where a bus to take us back to the town where we were staying awaited us.

What was strange was that during that wonderful holiday, which gave Marie-Claire great satisfaction, and precisely on that day when her joy had reached its climax, something happened to which I did not pay much attention at the time. It hurt me a little then, but as I look back at it now, it seems it was a sign of the end of my relationship with Marie-Claire.

After dinner, I left Marie-Claire to pore over her maps and travel books and headed, as usual, to the washbasins. I had hardly filled the basin with water when I saw her. She had just emerged from one of the shower rooms. I did not doubt for a second that she was Greek. She walked toward me as she combed her wet hair. When she came near, I smiled at her. She smiled back and continued walking. There was something whorish about her smile and clothes, and particularly the way she walked and moved her body; it unnerved and excited me at the same time.

I started washing the dishes, and as I was wondering if it would be a good idea to take a walk in her general direction to look for her after I had finished the dishes. I was surprised to find her coming back: not to wash dishes but to fill a jug with water. Again, she smiled at me when she passed by on her way to her tent. This time I left the dishes in the basin and followed her. I wanted to know where she was staying.

I got closer to her, focusing on her backside, which was practically bare. A few moments later, she turned and approached a tall man whom I had not noticed before. He was standing a few steps away from a large tent, with two children playing in front of it. He took the jug from her in a swift motion and stared at me, making it clear that he had noticed me following his woman.

I did not want to go back to where I had been, so as not to incriminate myself. I continued walking in the same direction, as if out for a stroll. When I reached the wall that surrounded the camp, I turned back and took a different path to the washbasins. I did not feel safe until I looked behind me and did not see the tall man.

Had it ended there, things would have been fine, but the problem was that the image of that woman moving her backside took complete hold of my mind. I had not desired a woman so strongly since I had met Marie-Claire. What was worse was that her image remained with me for the rest of the holiday, so much so that whenever I took Marie-Claire or whenever she took me, I felt that I was having sex with that Greek woman and not Marie-Claire. This left me with mixed emotions of pain and regret because I felt that I was betraying Marie-Claire. I did not succeed in breaking that woman's spell on me until the vacation was over and we had returned to Paris and were once again immersed in the city's rhythm.

15

focused my attention on the plants and I noticed that they had grown taller. Their leaves seemed greener in the morning sun. Marie-Claire leaned over the plants, with her back to me, so that she could feel the plant roots. I glimpsed part of her hips. Usually I did not hesitate or wait. I would approach her immediately and cling to her. She would understand that I desired to take her as she bent over the plants.

This time I contemplated her hips for a long while, as if seeing them for the first time. When I finally decided to get up and cling to her from behind, she pushed me away with one of her hands as she continued feeling the plant with the other. I clung to her again and she turned to face me. "I don't want to, do you understand?" She glared at me to make it clear that she was not joking. She went back to leaning over her plants.

It had only been a few months since we'd returned from Crete, but how far that holiday seemed from the days that followed it. Marie-Claire had treated me with tenderness and graciousness, responding to my every request, and sometimes yielding to any impulses that came to my mind.

I was not surprised by her rejection. I was sure that she knew, with her female intuition, that I did not really want her. Things like that could not be concealed from her. She must have noticed that my desire for her was not genuine, compulsive, and all-consuming as before; that I was just going through the motions. In any case, she did not like it when I approached her from behind as she leaned over the plants, especially in the mornings. What really bothered me was the way she rejected me. Everything about her rebuff suggested severity and repulsion: the motion of her hand as she pushed me away; the tone of her voice; and especially, her direct, cold, long glare. I had never been faced with that kind of rejection, even during fights when she abandoned me and would not let me near her in bed.

I remained silent. I wiped the breadcrumbs off the table and instead of throwing them into the garbage as usual, I opened the kitchen window and threw them out to the pigeons. I washed all the cups, spoons, and knives, and the coffee pot slowly and with pleasure, relishing the softness of the lemon-scented lather. I returned to the living room to bask in the sun and enjoy its warmth, for it rarely came out that time of year.

Marie-Claire was still in front of her plants. She had not moved. Indeed it seemed to me that she was bending even lower and that a larger part of her hips was bare. I wondered, as I went back to sit on the sofa, if she was doing that on purpose to arouse and annoy me at the same time, but I abandoned the idea shortly afterward, without being convinced of anything to the contrary.

I recalled the way she had moved her hand as she pushed me away, the tone of her voice, and her cold stare, which seemed to belong to some distant time, and I was more convinced that her rejection was truly harsh. The strange thing was that I was not as annoyed this time. What was more, deep down I felt I deserved such a treatment; for how could I wrong a woman who loved me by pretending to desire her so powerfully and spontaneously when all I really wanted was to penetrate her?

Marie-Claire straightened up. She turned around and looked at me. I smiled at her and she responded with a smile so faint, it was barely detectable on her lips, which still showed signs of sleep. I understood from that that she did not wish to let things get more complicated or to get to a point that neither of us wanted; that became even clearer as Marie-Claire sat down by my side to, like me, enjoy the warmth of the sunrays filtering into the living room.

We did not speak for the longest time. Occasionally, I would steal a glance at her. Her face was a little pale, and there was a certain slowness in her gait that I was not used to. She probably had not slept well the night before. Who knows, maybe nightmares had woken her several times during the night.

I usually got up before she did on weekends. As soon I opened my eyes, I would get out of bed and leave the room so as not to deprive her of the long morning lie-in that she loved. After washing, I would prepare breakfast, and then I would set the table and wait for her.

This time she got up before me. She stayed on her back in bed, her head resting on her crossed arms. When I was sure she was awake I stretched out my arm and put my hand on her shoulder. She turned to me; she held my hand and started stroking it. I, in turn, stroked her hand for a while. We then got out of bed and went to the kitchen.

Breakfast took a long time, as usual. Marie-Claire spoke of the lovely weather and she wished that it would remain so for the whole day. I spoke of the places we could visit, expressing a clear desire to go to one of the major museums, although I knew that Marie-Claire did not like museums, especially on weekends, because they filled up with flocks of tourists, as she put it.

The silence grew thicker. I felt I could not take it anymore, not just because it had gone on too long but also because it was deepening the rift between Marie-Claire and myself to the point that she seemed very distant, even though she was sitting mere inches away on the sofa. I felt that she was nervous, introverted, mysterious, and unreachable.

"The plants have grown taller," I said in an attempt to escape the heavy silence and the painful feeling it built up inside me. Marie-Claire moved her head slightly. "We had to be away from home for a long while for me to notice that," I added with false enthusiasm. Marie-Claire turned her head toward the plants and, for the first time, she did not seem beautiful to me as I observed her from that angle.

I got up and headed to the plants. I leaned over them. I started feeling their leaves and stems, exactly as Marie-Claire did. I did not usually do this, for my relationship with plants was different from hers. I would at most water them every now and again, or change their position so that they would not be deprived of the sunlight necessary for their growth. But this time, I felt drawn to the plants by a strong force. It was as if I was escaping to them from myself; as if I was relying on them to help me bear all the thoughts and feelings pervading me.

"Don't touch the leaves like that; do it gently and tenderly," said Marie-Claire loudly.

"Don't worry," I replied, without ceasing to feel the leaves.

"They are very delicate and you might pull them out if you keep touching them that way," Marie-Claire added heatedly.

I went back to my place on the sofa, feeling a little better because I had succeeded in forcing Marie-Claire to talk. I was not sure if the way I had handled the leaves would result in their being pulled out; it wasn't important that her voice still seemed harsh and her hand movements somewhat violent. What was important was that she had ceased to be silent and that I no longer saw her as withdrawn and distant.

As I searched for something to say to her to keep the silence from finding its way between us again, I heard her ask me if I was pleased with my students that year, and whether the university I had succeeded in convincing to give me a teaching contract was better than that of last year.

In truth I had not expected that from her at that point. I did not imagine that she was capable of thinking of such things, which concerned me alone, particularly in her state and particularly after my mistake in pretending that I desired her when all I wanted was to enter her the way I would any whore or woman with whom I had no relationship and toward whom I felt nothing: a woman that is transformed in a single unknowable moment into a wet hole that we plug in our quest for transient physical pleasure.

Her questions made me happy because they deepened my sense of calm and restored some sense of security to my perturbed soul. I grasped this rare opportunity and launched into a long conversation, as if avenging all my previous silence. I talked to her of the university, which was unlike all the universities I had taught at before. I told her about the beautiful libraries, the large gardens, the spacious halls with large windows. I spoke to her of the French teachers who asked me many, typically naive and unusual, questions, about the Arabic language, and about the others who asked me to write their names in Arabic on pieces of paper that they kept or threw in the trash after staring at them for a long time. I told her about the students whose attendance in my classes was irregular. I told her about their different nationalities, about their behavior during the lectures, about what I had discovered of their troubles and problems with relationships between boys and girls. I told her of the successful lectures and the disastrous ones. I told her of the students' admiration for the vagrant poets, and how they liked al-Saleek bin al-Salaka the best, like all the students I had lectured before.

Marie-Claire did not interrupt me. From time to time she lifted her head from the top of the sofa to look at me, indicating that she was listening attentively to what I was saying. When I stopped talking, she slid her body toward me so that she was almost glued to me. She lifted her arm and leaned over a little, exposing her underarm to me, but I felt no desire to smell it.

16

"Come, I want to show you something."
It had not been long since my return home. I was tired that day because I had worked until late afternoon at the hotel, then I had gone to the university where I had given two consecutive lectures that had taken a lot of effort. When I got home, I lay down on the sofa fully dressed. I did not even have the energy to take off my shoes.

"I will show you something, and then we will take a tour in the city," said Marie-Claire as she smiled. I stared at her face for a long moment, so she added in a comforting tone, "I am sure you will enjoy the tour. Now come and do not ask me about anything.'

The truth was, I was not about to ask her anything. I had no desire at all to talk at that point; I was also afraid of angering her if I did ask anything, because she was going through a rough patch for some unknown reason. She was very sensitive and would get upset easily and over the silliest things.

She ran down the stairs. I followed her silently. Once we were out of the building, she walked ahead for a few steps then stopped in front of a motorbike parked on the sidewalk near a tree. As she pointed to it, she asked, "What do you think?"

I stared at her in amazement. I did not understand anything until she said, as she got closer to the motorbike and grabbed the handlebars, "It's mine. I bought it an hour ago."

I knew that Marie-Claire liked cars, motorbikes, and bicycles. I think she inherited this passion from her father, who adored cars. She had mentioned many times before that she'd like to buy a motorbike to save her the agony of taking the metro, which she could no longer tolerate because, as she'd say, of its foul-smelling and depressing underground passageways. But it never occurred to me that she would one day buy such a big motorbike, one that only men could ride.

"But how will you ride it?"

"Don't worry, I have ridden bigger bikes," Marie-Claire answered, before taking out two helmets from a box at the back of the motorbike and handing one to me.

"Put it on your head."

"But . . . ."

"Don't worry, everything will be just fine," she interrupted, as she placed the helmet firmly on my head and secured the strap under my chin; she then pulled down the transparent plastic windshield to protect my face.

Marie-Claire got on to the front of the rectangular seat before revving up the engine. She then ordered me to climb on behind her. I placed myself on the back section of the seat, and when the motorbike took off, I grabbed her clothes for fear of falling to the ground and breaking my bones.

It was the first time I had ever been on a motorbike like that. It never occurred to me that I would do so some day. Gradually it picked up speed. My fear rose, so I clung to Marie-Claire even tighter. I enfolded her in my arms and leaned in on her with my whole body. She moved her torso and tried to push me further down the seat with her back to lessen the burden on her.

"Sit up straight and don't move."

Once we had traveled a short distance, my fear of falling diminished. I felt brave; I lifted my head and adjusted my position. Once I saw that everything was going smoothly, I stopped clinging to Marie-Claire and moved my hands to the back of the seat and held on to that. I then started watching the cars moving to our right and to our left. I looked at the drivers and passengers, who in turn looked at us.

"Still afraid?"

"No."

"What do you think? Do you like motorbikes?'

"They are not like cars."

We entered a long, less congested road. Marie-Claire increased the speed of the motorbike. She leaned over the handlebars even more as she pushed her backside backward, forcing me to shuffle a little so that she could have as much of the seat as possible. She stopped at the traffic lights, ahead of all the cars. As soon as the light turned green, the motorbike took off in a way that surprised me, even though Marie-Claire had warned me of what she intended to do; but what annoyed me was the racket the motorbike made as it sped off.

Some pedestrians stopped on the sidewalk and looked at us sharply; others raised their hands to object to the motorbike's noise. Marie-Claire moved her backside as though she were dancing. She laughed out loud. She was like a happy child who had just escaped punishment she deserved for a naughty deed.

We got to a big square that branched out into several streets. All the cars, buses, and trucks were either stopped or moving very slowly, due to the traffic. Marie-Claire reduced her speed but continued to move forward without stopping, penetrating the enormous swarm of cars and slithering smoothly between them.

"Nothing can stop you at times like this when you're on a motorbike," said Marie-Claire with not a little pride. Her voice got louder as the motorbike picked up speed after passing the square. "That's why I prefer motorbikes to cars; I feel freer."

I felt a measure of happiness as I watched Marie-Claire succeed in overtaking a large number of fancy cars and some of the big motorbikes driven by men, leaving them all far behind. I realized then that she was truly a good driver and I was overcome by pride in her. To express my admiration and pride, I tickled her back a little, and to reciprocate what had apparently made her feel good, she passed her hand over my thigh as she pushed her backside closer to me.

"Get ready; in a moment we're going to move to the circular highway that surrounds the city."

I was frightened once more, for the cars on these roads moved at reckless speeds, as though taking part in a crazy race, and the traffic never stopped. All accidents led to death, except in very rare cases. As if understanding the anxiety expressed by my silence, Marie-Claire added, "You know, the highway is safer than people think."

We traveled a long distance on the highway, then left it and headed home. Marie-Claire accelerated, and I felt as if we were flying. What was strange was that I never felt that I was in any danger, because I was so amazed and so completely engrossed with the speed that there was no room for fear.

On the way back we stopped near a car waiting for the green light. I noticed as I stole a glimpse at its driver—a middle-aged man of about fifty—that he was looking wide-eyed at Marie-Claire. Marie-Claire did not notice: her eyes were fixed on the traffic lights. I leaned over and whispered to her that it seemed a middle-aged man had fallen in love with her. When she turned to him, the middle-aged man gave her a wide smile and a big thumbs-up.

At other intersections I noticed that passengers would stare at us for a long time. Sometimes they smiled at us or nodded their heads as they looked fixedly at the motorbike. I did not pay them much attention. Sometimes I felt like returning their gaze, feeling proud that I was part of what had caught the attention of all these people.

Once home, I realized the secret behind all this attention, and my pride in myself diminished. I grasped that people had been staring at us because we'd presented a rather unfamiliar sight. It was usually men who drove such large motorbikes, leaving the back of the seat to women, not the other way around. That is why the middle-aged man had given Marie-Claire the thumbs-up, to express his admiration.

"Next time I will leave the driving to you," Marie-Claire said jokingly before heading to the kitchen. I sat on the sofa, feeling that the motorbike ride had rid me of the weariness that had threatened to overtake me before we left the house. When I started taking off my shoes, Marie-Claire said, as she came back into the living room, "Don't take your shoes off."

I looked at her in amazement, so she added as she leaned over and kissed me on the cheek like a mother trying to convince her child to do something against his will, "Do you think that such an event will take place just like that?"

"What event?"

"Buying the motorbike."

After planting another kiss on my cheek, she went on, "We must celebrate. And in any case we must go out because there is nothing to eat in the house; the fridge is completely empty."

"Which restaurant shall we go to?" I asked her as we headed to the door.

"A Moroccan one; it's nearby."

On our way to the restaurant, we passed the motorbike parked in front of the building. Marie-Claire stopped and inspected it for a long time and before we continued walking, she bent down to check that the thick chain used to prevent the motorbike from being stolen was securely fastened around the back wheel.

17

Everything about the restaurant where we had our dinner was exceptional.

The spaciousness that left you feeling safe and comfortable. The traditional Moroccan decor. The round tables that were far apart enough to allow for a conversation that did not resemble whispering and leave you feeling that everyone else was eavesdropping on everything you said. The soft traditional Moroccan music—Melhoun. And most importantly of all, the delicious food and the green mint tea of which we each had three cups—the last on the house as a gift from the owner, who did not stop smiling at us as we ate, and who kept asking if we were satisfied with their service.

I did not feel overwhelmed with annoyance the way I usually did when I entered a restaurant. From the first few moments, I felt that I was in a comfortable place, a restaurant completely unlike the others to which Marie-Claire had taken me. This feeling intensified as the owner escorted us to a corner table, which, as we discovered, was pleasantly located away from the entrance, but had a view of most of the tables.

Everything, then, was just right for us to spend a lovely evening during which we would be able to get closer to one another, particularly at a time when Marie-Claire was very sensitive, and maybe in light of the slight rift in our relationship, which I felt had begun to change and to lose some of its spontaneity since that morning when Marie-Claire had rebuffed me so harshly.

Everything would have been just right had it not been for the woman who fate decreed should sit directly in front of me at the table nearest to me. As soon as I laid eyes on her, I remembered the Greek woman I had seen near the wash-basins and shower rooms at the camping site in Crete; she resembled her a great deal.

I had no doubt that she was an Arab, specifically from the Maghreb region, even though I could not distinguish her accent from where I sat. I was not sure from which country exactly, but I believed her to be Tunisian, from somewhere inland such as Baja or al-Qasrayn. She smiled a lot and looked everywhere, and from time to time she would raise her hand to adjust her hair and reveal her underarm and the area around it. She was wearing a sleeveless shirt, with a bare neck and shoulders, which made me assume that the man sitting opposite her, with his back to me, was not her husband.

I stole several glances. Then I stopped. I looked at the other customers at the other tables, and to the street, trying to forget about her; I watched the waiters as they moved between the tables; I looked at the plates they carried; I asked Marie-Claire many questions about the motorbike to get her to talk; but it was all in vain. I felt drawn to the woman, for in her eyes and her movements was something that reminded me of the Greek woman at the camping site.

When she noticed me looking at her, she started looking back at me, furtively, like me. Sometimes she would smile at me as she turned to look at the street. I returned her smile very cautiously during the moments when Marie-Claire turned around to look at the customers leaving or entering the restaurant, to call the waiter to ask for something, or to see what was on other people's plates, which she loved to do at every restaurant we went to.

The woman suddenly got up and pushed her chair back quickly, making a lot of noise and drawing everyone's attention. With an exaggeratedly feminine movement she took her handbag, which was on the table, and turned toward the washrooms. I watched her as she moved slowly with her back straight until she disappeared behind the door. As soon as I turned my head back, Marie-Claire asked me, "Do you like her?"

"Who?"

"Who?! The woman you were staring at."

I was dumbfounded, tongue-tied, embarrassed, and also proud, for this was one of those rare occasions when Marie-Claire seemed undoubtedly jealous of another woman. This feeling was confirmed when she added, as if to curse, "She's a whore."

I wasn't convinced; I don't know why. All I knew was that something deep inside me told me she wasn't a whore. But I didn't dare open my mouth. Marie-Claire continued, as though she'd realized what was going on in my head, "She moves like a whore; her glances, too."

The woman came out of the washroom and returned to her place, looking around. Marie-Claire fixed on her as if wanting to know what woman had dared challenge her and steal me from her right before everyone's eyes.

"She's a whore; look at the way she's looking at the men."

I remained silent. Marie-Claire also went silent. I realized from the cold and direct glares she threw at me every now and again that my behavior, which seemed to have shocked her, not only offended but also insulted her. That made me even more nervous.

At that moment, after stopping the Melhoun tape playing in the background, the owner announced that there was going to be a party at the restaurant, and that we would be entertained by a singer and a dancer whom he described as famous stars. I had never heard of either of them, however, even though I occasionally listened to Arab radio stations, and read with some interest and enjoyment the latest news about singers in any Arabic magazine or newspaper that came my way.

When the singer began to sing, Marie-Claire turned her whole body to face the small platform where the musical group was seated and started listening as she looked at the group. When the beat picked up, she began clapping with the others, swaying with her head and body in a way that showed she was enjoying the music. I found that a little strange, because I knew that she was not fond of Arabic music, which she found slow and boring.

And even though I did not like a thing about the singer—not his voice, his appearance, his movements, or even his smile, I tried to appear like Marie-Claire. When she turned to me, I clapped, shook my shoulders, and nodded my head as though I were enjoying myself. All I wanted at that moment was to forget that woman, or to at least give the impression that I was trying to forget her, and to do whatever I thought would please Marie-Claire, to help her overcome her feelings of being slighted and offended.

The singer disappeared after a couple of songs, none of which I liked, because they all belonged to the kind of music often played at restaurants and nightclubs. The dancer entered the dance floor, taking her place amid a storm of applause and shouts of admiration. Marie-Claire watched with great interest. The dancer returned the warm welcome by blowing copious kisses to the crowd. Then she started to dance.

Unlike most dancers I had seen, she delighted me from the start. She seemed beautiful from where I was seated. In fact, I had rarely seen a dancer so beautiful. But what I really liked most about her was the way she danced. She did every-thing dancers did, but with elegance and without being taw-dry. There was something about the way she moved that was both demure and shy, and this awarded her a special kind of beauty.

Marie-Claire continued to smile as she looked at the dancer and at two men who, apparently unable to overcome their desire to dance, got onto the dance floor and began undu-lating around the dancer, oblivious to the cold glares from the restaurant owner, and the customers' hissing.

A while later, a French woman got onto the dance floor. She approached the dance floor and danced with one of the two men in a way that indicated they were acquainted. More women felt encouraged, including the one who looked like the woman from the camping site. They got onto the dance floor. Suddenly, Marie-Claire got up, and, without saying a word, she joined them.

That did not bother me, for even though she danced in a strange way, it was still exciting. I knew that she loved to dance. What was more, I was relieved because I no lon-ger felt surrounded, and that my every look and move were under scrutiny. I was also sure that dancing would make her happy, which in turn would help her forget the matter of the woman, and perhaps deliver us from the rough patch we were going through.

Marie-Claire made huge, obvious efforts to make her dancing appear eastern. I noticed that she kept getting closer to the dancer, to try to ape her movements; unfortunately, that only made her dancing seem even stranger, as she was mostly unable to make the right movements. Her body, which was unused to this kind of dance, did not cooperate. It refused to give in to her desires. I felt some pity for her as I watched her trying hard to be like the Arab women. That feeling heightened when I noticed that some people at nearby tables were poking fun at her.

An Arab man, who had caught my attention with the way he danced, approached her. It was obvious that he was trying to make his dancing as masculine as possible. He leaned toward her and smiled at her, but instead of moving away from him as the other women he encircled did, she remained in her place. Not only that, but she returned his smile with a wide smile of her own, and when he mustered the courage to dance with her, with his eyes fixed on her body, she quickly complied.

But what really hurt was that when he took her hand she got so close to him that she was almost glued to him; and in an even bolder move, he put his hand on her shoulder and she let him. She threw me a glance every now and then to let me know that she was doing this on purpose to provoke me. I realized then that she was much more offended and insulted than I had initially thought.

I did not comment on her behavior when she came back to her seat. She asked me if I'd enjoyed what I'd seen. I nodded affirmatively. I had a strong urge, before we left the restaurant, to look at the woman who looked like the woman from the camping site but I was determined not to do so. We walked silently and slowly until we reached our building. Marie-Claire went to the motorbike to check the chain. She then passed her hand tenderly over the seat and asked me, "It's beautiful, isn't it?"

I did not reply.

18

I won't deny that I felt some measure of joy when Marie-Claire announced that her mother was not feeling well and that she had decided to travel to the country, not only because she would be away for a whole week, but also because she would spend a long time with her mother, whom she had not been to see for over two years. This would surely be an opportunity for them to get closer and understand one another better, something I had always secretly hoped for because of what I felt was a flaw in their relationship.

It was the first time since I had known her that Marie-Claire would be away from home for a whole week. It was also the first time since her father had died that she would spend all this time with her mother in the country. At first she was not eager to travel; later she tried to shorten the length of her stay. But, uncharacteristically, her mother insisted: she called her several times and at different times of day over a short period, managing to convince her that her health had taken a sudden turn for the worse and required that she visit her for a whole week at least.

I made the most of this completely unexpected opportunity to take my life back to its earlier rhythm. I returned temporarily to my previous untidiness, and I succumbed to laziness and lethargy. It had been a long time since I'd been alone in the house, free to do whatever I wanted without feeling that I was being watched. It had been a long time since I had experienced the kind of solitude I had known before meeting Marie-Claire. For that reason I was very keen to live it deeply; to make the most of it and enjoy it as much as I could.

The first days of the week passed slowly and uneventfully. When I was not working, I spent most of my time at home. I was in a good mood. Nothing disturbed my thoughts or occupied my mind. No anger, no tension. No conversations, discussions, or fights. Nothing but silence and tranquillity. I did not even give in to my trick of remembering the past, which I sometimes liked to indulge in at times like these, for fear it might awaken feelings and thoughts that would spoil my solitude.

I had no doubt that I would spend all the days of the week in that state of tranquillity, calm, and rapture at my solitude. But on the fourth day I discovered that I was completely wrong, and that there was nothing more mysterious, complicated, and unpredictable than the relationship between a man and a woman! For from the moment I got up I was aware of the image of Marie-Claire occupying my mind. I tried to get rid of it by thinking of important issues, but I could not. After a while, a strange and at first unfamiliar sensation took me by surprise, that of missing Marie-Claire; I found myself truly pining for her.

During the fifth day, my longing for her increased. When I woke up and stretched my arm only to feel it fall on her cold, bare spot, I felt my yearning had reached its peak. That was when I became aware, with some degree of astonishment, of the importance of her presence in the house, and of how much I needed her!

In an attempt to free myself, or at least lessen the heavy effect of these sensations that occupied my soul I know not how, I engrossed myself in reciting verses of my favorite vagrant poets out loud. I listened to almost all of the Arabic music I had. I replied to letters I had received a long time ago but ignored; one of these was a long letter from my sister, chastising me harshly because the money I had sent her to repair my mother's grave, which had almost been swept away by recent floods, had been insufficient. I left the house and took long walks, attracting the attention of several passersby by talking loudly to myself.

One day, before she returned, I could not sleep all night. Her image refused to leave me. It didn't matter whether I kept the lights on or switched them off to plunge the bedroom into darkness, or whether I closed my eyes or kept them open to fix my gaze on what was around me. The strange thing was that the more I felt her presence, the farther away her face seemed to become, and the hazier its details, to the extent that what remained of her face, as recalled by memory at that point in time, was very little.

This was not the first time I had found myself unable to recall a familiar face; it had happened to me several times before with faces that were quite different from each other. Usually I would occupy myself with other things in order to forget the face completely and expel it from my mind. When I would return later, I often found that my memory could recall it completely, in all its details. But this time I was unable to do so, because Marie-Claire's image did not leave me for an instant.

I sprang out of bed and looked around, but I could not find pictures of Marie-Claire anywhere: not on the small bedside table; not on any of the bookshelves; not on the stereo player; and not on the low cabinet in the apartment entrance. This was because, like me, Marie-Claire did not like enlarging her photographs and putting them in pretty frames around the apartment as most people did, particularly because she didn't think she looked beautiful in such photographs. Contrary to what I and almost everyone who knew her thought, Marie-Claire believed that she was not photogenic.

The only place in the flat where I might have found a photograph of Marie-Claire was inside what we had jokingly nicknamed 'the cupboard.' The 'cupboard' was made up of three cardboard boxes of the same color and size, and was hidden from view in the last drawer of the small cabinet we kept at the entrance to the apartment. From the very first day that Marie-Claire moved in with me I understood that the 'cupboard' was out of bounds to me, and that under no circumstances must I peek at its contents or even open it. Although we were living under the same roof, it was important for Marie-Claire to have her own space in the house: a place for herself alone that I could not enter; a closed, secret place where she could have some privacy. "For where is the value and flavor of life," she would always say, "without a little privacy?"

But this did not mean that Marie-Claire kept the contents of her 'cupboard' secret from me; from the start she told me what she kept in it: letters, pictures, and various other things dating back to her childhood and teens; she even showed me a picture of herself wearing a nun's habit on her first communion and the gold chain she received as a gift on that occasion. It is just that she did not wish me to invade her private world and poke my nose in her personal things.

I knew all that and was fully aware of it, but this damned desire which had overwhelmed me was too difficult to contain, especially during those critical, shadowy moments between sleep and wakefulness. What made me take a quick decision to embark on something I had dared not do before was my resolve to do only what was necessary. Only one thing alone was important to me—to find a recent photo of

Marie-Claire as quickly as possible and with a minimum of disturbance to the contents of 'the cupboard.'

I approached 'the cupboard' and opened the last drawer, hoping that I would find what I was looking for in the first box, which would undoubtedly relieve me of the feeling of guilt that overcame me the moment I saw the three boxes neatly arranged one on top of the other in a corner of the drawer. Luckily, that was exactly what happened. The first thing that caught my eye after I'd removed the lid of the box was a small album whose cover and general appearance indicated that it was old. I opened it eagerly and began to turn its pages. There were pictures of her mother, of herself as a child and as a toddler, alone, or with her father, her mother, or both. There were also a few pictures of old people, whom I guessed to be grandparents, but most of the pictures were of her father. Some were very old, and he seemed like a happy and handsome young man. There was one picture of him wearing an army uniform and I discerned from the background that it was taken in Algeria.

I did not find any recent pictures of Marie-Claire until the last page of the album. I removed it slowly and carefully from under the transparent paper. After sitting on the sofa and switching on the side lamp, I placed the photograph on my knee and contemplated the face as though I had never seen it before, and for the first time I became aware that Marie-Claire had been right about what she'd always said about her pictures: that she was more beautiful in real life.

After examining the picture, I put it back in its place. The moment I closed the album I caught a glimpse of something I had not seen when I had taken out Marie-Claire's album; something that caused me to panic from the moment I caught sight of it with only passing interest. It was a small photograph that seemed to have been removed from an ID card, as it still bore evidence of an old stamp in the corner.

I had no doubt that it was of Ladislaus, the first person Marie-Claire loved. In the picture he seemed a gentle child, but I did not find him appealing, even though his face was somewhat attractive and charming. I stared at his delicate lips, which were pursed as those of one who was not used to sitting in front of the camera. And when I thought of him using them to kiss Marie-Claire's lips several times, jealousy awoke in me once again.

I felt that I was dull and stupid. A painful feeling of self-disgust welled up inside of me, for how could I be jealous of an innocent child such as this, who hardly seemed to know how to blow his own nose, simply because he had kissed Marie-Claire years ago in a basement full of mice?

I put the album back into the box. As I leaned over the three boxes to rearrange them carefully, I heard a sound; something like a ticking sound. I leaned closer to the drawer and the ticking became clearer. I moved the boxes aside only to realize that what I had thought to be the bottom of the drawer was in fact a thick cardboard layer. I removed it quickly only to be astonished at what I saw. Watches of all types and sizes were piled up in the bottom of the drawer: twenty-three to be exact. I knew that Marie-Claire loved watches the way she loved shoes, of which she owned a great many. I had not imagined, though, that she would have so many watches, especially as she the ones she kept were mostly faulty or so old that she would probably never wear them, just as her mother kept empty champagne bottles and shiny wrapping paper.

I was even more astonished when I opened the small round box made of Chinese bamboo that was hidden among the watches to discover that it was full of rings, earrings, and necklaces. Marie-Claire was not one of those women who loved jewelry; I had rarely seen a ring on her fingers or earrings on her ears.

I closed the drawer and went back to the bedroom. I got myself firmly into bed and closed my eyes. But the image of Ladislaus with his delicate pursed lips persisted in my mind, and instead of helping me forget how much I missed Marie-Claire, it made me miss her even more, after the feeling had lessened when I'd mulled over her picture and searched her boxes. Even worse, I was overcome by a strong desire to hear her voice at that very moment.

I looked at the alarm clock. It was not as late as I had imagined. Marie-Claire would probably still be in the living room and would not have gone to bed yet. But the problem was that I did not want her to know that I missed her that much, and even if I found a convincing way to call her at that time my voice would surely give me away. In any case she would know with her female intuition.

After much exhausting hesitation I got out of bed and headed to the living room. I did not switch on any lights, as though I did not want to see the telephone; as though I did not want to see my hands stretching toward it; as though the darkness would help me tolerate what I could no longer tolerate. I did not sit as I usually did when making a call. I remained standing like a forgotten pole. With a brisk movement I lifted the receiver as I leaned over the telephone table. I dialed the number. I even stopped breathing. "Hello, hello? Who is calling? Hello?" I did not reply. I moved the phone away from my ear because I could no longer bear to hear her voice. Then I collapsed on the sofa.

19

I realized from the moment our eyes met that she knew it was I who had telephoned her the previous day without daring to speak, but contrary to what I expected, she seemed neither annoyed nor upset. In fact she seemed rather pleasant. Had she gathered from my strange silence over the telephone, and especially from the warm welcome I could not hide, that I had missed her and that I was still attached to her despite everything that had happened in our relationship since that morning when she had so harshly spurned me? Had the distance allowed her to realize that her behavior had been apathetic, brusque, careless, and neglectful? Had the trip helped her see things more clearly and in a different light? Or had spending a whole week in a distant village with her mother calmed her nerves so much that she had returned to her old ways?

All I knew was that this absence gave me back my real Marie-Claire; the tender, innocent, spontaneous Marie-Claire. After a long time and in certain delicate circumstances I was able to see once again that joyful face which radiated a mixture of familiarity, spontaneity, and calmness. What was strange was that all this happened much more quickly than even in my wildest dreams. It was as if we had never fought, or had an unspoken prior agreement to forget suddenly and once and for all everything that had been tearing us apart in the past few months.

"Come," said Marie-Claire as she took my hand and pulled me to the table onto which she had piled up her bags.

"Look what I brought from the countryside," she added with some pride before she began to empty the bags and pile their contents on the table. "All these are presents from my mother's farmer neighbors."

Vegetables, cheeses, sausages, eggs, cherry and quince marmalade, minced pork, cooked rabbit. Marie-Claire's eyes darted between the table and myself; she could not stop smiling. I smiled, too, and I looked with interest at everything she brought with her from the country, nodding my head in admiration to share her joy.

"I never imagined that farmers could be so nice!" she said as she raised some of the cheeses to her nose to smell them. I felt the urge to do the same, but instead of smelling some cheese, I sniffed a potato that had caught my attention because of its shape and large size. Suddenly she placed the cheeses on the table and said as she leaned over the large bag that was still open, "I forgot; there is something else I got from the country." She took out a large bunch of flowers, removed the wrapping, and brought them close to my nose. "Smell these."

I buried my nose in the bunch of flowers and exhaled the aromatic fragrance as I closed my eyes to express my pleasure

"Do you recognize the scent?"

I nodded as I continued sniffing the flowers.

"What is it?" asked Marie-Claire, in the tone of one examining her students.

I had no doubt at all that I'd smelled that scent several times before, but I was unable to answer. I opened my eyes and looked at the flowers intimating that this would help me remember their name. In truth I was deceiving both myself and Marie-Claire. I was sure that I would not remember the name even if I spent a whole hour staring at the flowers because my knowledge of the names of plants, trees, and flowers was as weak as my knowledge of the names of unfamiliar birds, insects, and animals.

"Lilacs," said Marie-Claire, before adding, as she leaned over me bringing her breasts closer to my face, "I picked them from a tree in my mother's garden."

I became aware of the scent of the lilacs changing into another scent. There was something in the air with which it mixed and blended. I realized as I sniffed my surroundings that it was the scent of Marie-Claire. I rarely detected it so strongly. Perhaps she had sweated more than usual as she carried her bags and suitcases. But my nose, which had been excited from the moment Marie-Claire piled everything she had got from the country on the table, was not repulsed by this unusual aroma of lilac mingled with the scent of a woman's sweaty body. In fact, it found it delicious, actually exciting and provocative.

Marie-Claire put the lilacs in the ceramic vase that I'd given her as a gift a long time ago. As I watched her arranging the flowers as she did with her plants, and then placing the vase on a shelf in the bookcase, I remembered that she had admired the vase a great deal, and that she still considered it to be one of the most beautiful things I had ever got her from Tunis. I had also, in recent months, noticed that she only put flowers in the vase when she was happy with me.

Within minutes, Marie-Claire put an end to all the chaos she had created in the living room since her arrival. She tidied up and put everything back in its place. She left nothing on the table except some of the meat and cheese she had brought with her from the country so that we could have them for dinner, which she wanted to be country-like that evening, she said.

We sat close together at the table. We did not use plates, forks, spoons, or knives. Marie-Claire opened a bottle of wine. With a slow, deliberate movement she took out the small knife she had inherited from her father and began slicing the sausages. She gave me some and ate some herself with obvious relish.

I had no desire to eat at that time, and I do not like pork, especially sausages of any kind, but I did not refuse anything Marie-Claire offered me. Gradually, and after several sips of wine, I began eating the pork with such relish that it drew Marie-Claire's attention. She watched me both with admiration and with amazement. In all the years I had spent in that city, I had never eaten such a variety of pork meat as I did that night.

When we finished eating, Marie-Claire stretched out on the sofa. She closed her eyes and remained silent. I did not move. I remained still so as not to disturb her. After several long moments she started talking without moving or opening her eyes. She talked a little about her mother's sickness, which could be terminal. I noticed that she did not mention the name of the disease. It occurred to me to ask her about it, but I did not. Afterward she told me about the village where she'd spent a whole week: its old houses, its farmers, its big fields, the rhythm of life there.

All of a sudden she turned to lie on her side, facing me. With a strange smile on her lips that made me uncomfortable, she asked, "How about you, what did you do all week?"

"I went to work at the hotel as usual and I taught at the university." After a while, I could not stop myself from adding nervously, "And I waited for you."

"You waited for me?"

"Yes."

"All week?"

I did not know what to say, so I satisfied myself with giving her an enigmatic nod. I felt that what I'd said had warmed her heart a little, yet I could not find the courage to return her gaze. I got up and headed to the window to look for the plane tree that was surrounded by all the buildings.

"I missed you, too."

I turned to her only to find her that she had returned to her earlier position. She went quiet again. I stared into the darkness for a while, but I could not make out anything of the plane tree. I returned to the table. I collected whatever food was left on the table and carried it to the kitchen to put it in the fridge.

When I returned to the living room I found that Marie-Claire had taken off all her clothes and was lying naked on the sofa. She smiled at me when she saw me approaching her and taking off my clothes, too. She moved back to make room for me to lie down next to her. She stretched out her arm for me to put my head on it. She brought her head closer to mine so that our heads were almost touching. She looked fixedly at my face for a long time, with what looked like a smile on her lips. Then she started kissing me.

We did not get off the sofa until the morning. We also did not sleep. It was as if we were afraid that if we slept a little we would lose these rare, pleasurable feelings that we had not known for a long while. We did not say much. The glances, smiles, and caresses were far more eloquent than words. In the morning Marie-Claire prepared a delicious breakfast that we ate slowly and with great pleasure, exactly as we used to do at the start of our relationship.

But this did not last long. It was more like a beautiful short dream. It was more like that last, powerful glow of an ember before it is extinguished forever. A few days later, boredom and routine crept back into our relationship. We went back to fighting, most of the time over the silliest of things. Gradually, the apathy and brusqueness also found their way back into our relationship. For the first time I began to question whether I still loved Marie-Claire and whether she, too, still loved me.

20

had not touched Marie-Claire for a long time. Not because she'd rejected me, which happened sometimes and which I tolerated with some measure of wisdom and patience, but because I could no longer bear the expression that had started to peek through her eyes every time I came near her. It was as though she was saying, as she offered me her cold body, "Take me if you will; I won't object, but you won't get anything from me because I won't give you anything." Even so, I did not decide to go there; everything that happened and how I ended up there was just a coincidence.

I left the hotel, but instead of heading back home, I walked slowly, moving from one street to another, oblivious to the direction I was going. There was no particular place to which I wanted to go. I just did not want to go home at that time; I wanted to delay my return as much as possible so that I would not see Marie-Claire. I had no desire to see her, to talk to her, or even to look at her face because of the mockery and animosity I had detected in her voice the day before.

I do not know how I got there. My feet led me to a place I had never thought of visiting even when times were really bad. I do not even remember the names of the streets or the squares I crossed. All that I knew was that I suddenly found myself in Rue Saint Denis where the prostitutes were. I found myself right in front of them. Face to face.

I smiled as I looked at them. At first, the situation in which I found myself was embarrassing. It had been a long time since I had seen prostitutes of this kind because I had not stepped inside a whorehouse since I had come to live in this city. I later overcame my feelings of embarrassment and nervousness. A strange desire for these erect bodies, lining both sides of the street and standing in front of the buildings displaying themselves to passersby, was gradually awakened in me: a desire for Arab flesh combined with something akin to nostalgia for the whorehouses I had visited in my youth.

I strolled to the end of the street on the same sidewalk, then I walked back to the beginning on the opposite sidewalk. The area was very crowded at that time of night. Most of the open cafés and restaurants were packed with people. The slow-moving cars stopped from time to time so that the drivers could get a slow glance at the bodies on display. The noises that came from every direction were mixed with the smell of food, perfume, sweat, urine, tobacco, and alcohol. There were some tourists, who were wide-eyed, shinning with desire. Some of them planted themselves in front of building entrances, staring long at the whores of all kinds and all types, whose faces were painted with make-up that shone beneath the lights, their flimsy, see-through clothes leaving only little to the imagination.

I stopped at the head of the street. I remained there for several long moments as I looked absent-mindedly at passersby. I was uncertain what I should do. Should I give in to the call of my lust and to this desire, which did not diminish despite all the sagging, tired bodies I saw, and despite all the vulgar words I heard? Or should I leave the place immediately as my mind was commanding me to do?

I noticed from a quick glance behind me that there was a man standing one step away from me. When our eyes met he smiled at me, so I smiled back instinctively and I went back to looking at passersby. But I was surprised a moment later to find him standing right next to me. He smiled at me again. I understood from his smile this time that he wanted to ask me something, so I turned to him, indicating that I was ready to help him out. He slowly leaned over his head and asked in a low voice, "Do you suck?"

I did not understand his question, and I thought that I did not hear him properly.

"Suck? Suck what?"

He focused on my face. Suddenly he pulled out his tongue and licked his lips. Then he said flirtatiously and coyly before walking away, "Too bad you do not suck; I am good at sucking."

I understood everything as I watched him walk away, shaking his backside in a way that was intended to attract attention. He crossed the street and stood on the sidewalk opposite me, and leaned against one of the posts. Every so often he raised his hand in a slow effeminate movement to his head to play with his hair while looking at me in a way that let me know he had not completely given up on me.

I thought to myself as I left the place that all I needed that night was to have sex with a gay man. A few steps later I found myself facing the Rue Saint Denis prostitutes again. I decided not to answer the call of my lust, contrary to what my head was telling me, but my profound sexual desire, no doubt taking advantage of my preoccupation with the gay man, made the decision for me and led me there.

I took another round in the street looking for Arab prostitutes. It was not hard to find them, for I relied not only on their facial features but also on the way they spoke French, and on the fact that some Arabic escaped their lips, usually vulgar, swear words which made their clients laugh and attracted more than repulsed them.

After a detailed inspection of the bodies and faces, and some long comparisons, I made up my mind. I confidently approached a prostitute in her forties who smoked non-stop and who winked at everyone who looked at her just like the whores at common brothels. She was an average-looking Moroccan woman, with a wide chest, huge breasts, full hips, and three gold teeth that shone in the streetlight every time she opened her mouth.

It was not her voluptuous body that made me choose her; there were many bodies like hers, some that were sexier and better proportioned. Rather it was her dark skin and particularly her Bedouin face and that tattoo on her forehead. It had been a long time since I had seen a face like that, and I did not expect to find it at such a place because I had not imagined that Arab prostitutes like her worked the Rue Saint Denis.

"We are blessed by your visit," she said to me when I smiled at her, thereby confirming that I wanted her and not her colleague who was standing next to her. She asked me if I had a lot of money. I nodded several times to reassure her. She examined me from head to toe as if trying to discern from my appearance and clothes the kind of man I was. She then mentioned the amount I had to pay her later. When I nodded in agreement she instructed me to follow her.

"Come, oh come, my sweet darling."

We didn't do it in the building entrance she'd stood in before, as I'd expected; instead, we entered through a small side door. We walked through a long, narrow passage with a low ceiling from which hung a light bulb that was barely enough to light the place. We then climbed up an old, endless wooden staircase. We stopped after a while to catch our breath. I took the opportunity to place my hand fully on her hips to feel their weight. She let me do so slowly, which inflamed my desire for her even more.

"Algerian?" she asked me, when we started climbing again.

"No, Tunisian."

"All the Tunisians I know are fags. They get fucked like women."

She laughed, so I laughed, too, as I felt my pockets to make sure that my money was still there. I discovered that my official papers were not in a safe place so I moved them quickly to an inside pocket of my jacket and closed it tightly.

We changed direction, which implied that we were in a hotel. All the doors on the left and right were closed except for one from which we could see a man with Asian features; he watched us brazenly until we entered one of the rooms.

"The dirhams first," she said, as she extended her open hand toward me. She counted the cash I gave her loudly and obviously. She then examined the money for a long time to make sure that it was not counterfeit because, she said, Arabs, the sons of bitches, cheat a lot. When she finished, she hid the money in a small box that she placed under the carpet in the corner of the room. She then lay on the bed and spread open her thighs after taking off her underwear.

At that moment I truly understood what was in store for me. I had intended to ask her to bare her chest completely so that I could get a good look at her huge breasts. In fact I had been willing to pay her extra in return for her getting completely naked, but I changed my mind when I found myself face to face with her naked lower body and her organ, which was splayed out before me in contrived generosity.

"Come, come and fuck the pussy," she added in a cold, unfriendly tone when she noticed that I was taking my clothes off a little too slowly. "Come quickly, come."

I felt my desire waning fast, not only because of the way in which she displayed her body, but also because of her unfriendliness, which I did not expect from a woman, even if that woman were a whore. But I neither retreated nor withdrew. I was determined to follow through with the adventure I had started right to its end.

I got on the bed. She pulled me over with one hand and held my organ with the other. She put it below her belly and started moving her body. After a short while she asked me, "What's wrong with you? Why aren't you getting an erection?"

She closed her eyes. She lifted her lower body to increase the pressure on me. She started moving again and faking a few moans to excite me, but it didn't work. I took the opportunity of being on top of her to get a good look at her face.

I noticed something strange that made me freeze on the spot; the tattoo on her forehead looked exactly like the one I had seen on my mother's forehead in my dream.

When she noticed that everything she did to excite had no effect, she pushed me away with her hand. She got up and jeered, "I told you Tunisians were fags."

I got dressed hurriedly and left immediately. Once outside in the street, I walked quickly and did not slow down until I was far away from Rue Saint Denis. I found myself in a deserted place with poor lighting; the streets were short and narrow, and there were no cars at all. Every now and then a few homeless people passed by talking loudly or cursing the world and everyone in it. I proceeded to another street and stopped in front of some shop windows to take a peek at what was inside. When I felt that I could no longer walk, out of sheer weariness, I decided to go home.

I slowly opened the door to the flat. I did not turn the lights on. I took off my shoes and walked on tiptoe because I'd noticed that the bedroom door was ajar. Marie-Claire had no doubt not closed it as usual because she wanted to know what time I got home. I stretched out on the sofa without taking my clothes off. I closed my eyes and tried to sleep, but I could not. The image of the tattoo I had seen on the Moroccan whore's forehead would not leave me.

As I glanced around the living room I noticed that everything was not as clear as it usually was at that time of night. This upset me because often simply looking at my surroundings, from paintings to books and furniture helped to bear delicate situations like this. I was certain that the tattoo that reminded me both of my mother and the Moroccan whore at one and the same time would not fade easily from my memory so long as I remained in that darkness.

I thought over this dilemma for some time. I tried long and hard to shake off this pressing problem, but I failed to find a way to expel the image of the tattoo from my head without resorting to switching on the lights, thus risking waking Marie-Claire up and complicating matters even more. What was truly torturing me was that every time I thought of the tattoo I felt more pain. Gradually I gave in and convinced myself that I deserved this punishment, and that there was some justice to what was happening to me.

21

As soon I lay next to her on the bed she put out the light after shooting me a look, which I took to mean that she was upset that I had invaded her private space. She dragged her body to the edge of the bed and turned her back to me. She was completely naked. It had been a long time since I'd seen her like that. I turned to the opposite side. I buried my head in the pillow and began thinking about the verses I had read of the vagrant poets, and the topics I should focus on in the next day's lecture so that I could get rid of the image of her, which had taken over my thoughts. But my body would not obey and betrayed me this time. I looked long and hard at her body, at the curves I could clearly discern now that my eyes had become accustomed to the darkness, and I was overcome with desire.

It was obvious that my entering the bedroom, and at that time, came as a surprise to Marie-Claire because I had been sleeping on the sofa in the living room for quite a while by then, not just to get away from her, but also because I wanted to be alone and free. I would listen to Arabic radio; I would read; I would move the way I wanted to move; I would do what I wanted; and I would not sleep until I really felt like sleeping. And if it so happened that I decided to sleep next to her in bed, I would not usually enter the room until very late at night; in other words, after Marie-Claire had fallen fast asleep.

I focused again on her backside, which was only a few inches away and my excitement grew. Was she lying naked and in this position, which she knew excited me, in order to test me and test my ability to resist? Maybe she wanted me to fall into the trap, so that when I came closer to her, weak and submissive, she could turn me away harshly to make me suffer, or maybe she would react in an unexpected way in order to humiliate me.

Here was a woman I knew very well, and who knew me equally well. We were sleeping in the same bed and under the same roof as though we were married, and I desired her deeply. There she was lying completely naked next to me with her hips exposed in a way that was irresistible, and yet I could not even touch her. Were I to react like any man from Makhaleef I would have thrown her down on the bed, spread her thighs wide apart by force, and penetrated her violently the moment I had seen her, thus answering the Bedouin call inside me. Were I to tell any of the Makhaleef men what was happening to me at that moment, they would ridicule and mock me, saying I'd become as delicate as a woman as a result of being over-urbanized. How else would a woman dare lie naked in front of me and in this licentious way, a mere few inches away while I failed to ride her as only a stud could?

I could of course try. I could put my hand on her hip, slowly caress her upper back, or play with her hair to announce that I wanted her at that moment. But the problem was that her almost inevitable refusal would complicate matters; for what I was really afraid of was that it would arouse me so much that I would lose control.

I felt hot. I wiped the sweat collecting on my forehead with my hand. I tossed and turned in bed. Then I thought after a while how my constant movement might prevent her from sleeping or wake her up if she had already fallen asleep. I left the bedroom for the living room. I stood in the middle of the living room, in the darkness, for a long time, not knowing what to do. I went to the window to look through the curtains onto the street; then I went to the kitchen to make sure that the water and gas taps were securely shut. I did that even though I knew that they were shut.

When I returned to the bedroom I found that she'd changed position: she was lying on her back and her thighs were slightly open allowing me to see her sexual organ somewhat clearly. I could not move from nervousness and excitement. I closed my eyes and my hand reached instinctively to my lower belly. At that moment I remembered the small church I had been to visit before coming home—a small, beautiful Orthodox church. I had passed it several times before, but that was the first time I had entered it. It had been empty except for an old man seated on one of the front benches. A silence, both heavy and comfortable, reigned in the place. I looked at the paintings on its walls for a while before sitting on one of the benches in the back row as I usually did when I visited churches. I closed my eyes to better enjoy the silence. Before leaving, I did something I had never done before. I left a coin in a box and I lit a candle for my mother.

I moved my hand away from my lower belly. I turned my head to look at Marie-Claire. I listened for a long while to her breathing; when I was sure she was fast asleep I pulled the covers that were folded under her feet and I covered her lower body, believing that this would dampen my arousal. But, after a little while, I realized this was not working. If anything, I can say that her body, with its lower part now covered with a thin sheet, seemed even more enticing than before.

As I was wondering if it would be better for me, having reached this level of arousal, to uncover her lower half, Marie-Claire mumbled something as she moved her head on the pillow, and with a quick and sudden movement she turned to her side, pushing the cover to the edge of the bed with her feet. As I looked at her backside I thought how much closer to me it seemed after she had changed position.

I closed my eyes again; I buried my head in the pillow despite the heat. I remained still for a few moments, trying not to think of anything so that I could sleep. But I was surprised to find my hand wandering again toward my lower belly. I realized then that the best way to alleviate the pressures of this uncontrollable desire was to discharge it. Nothing would extinguish this raging fire inside my body except that secret habit which I had not indulged in since I had known Marie-Claire. But where should I do it? There, in the bedroom; in the living room; or in the bathroom? Or perhaps somewhere else? How would I dispose of the liquid that would be ejaculated from my organ and splatter all around me? Should I rush to the bathroom and wash calmly? Or should I wipe it with whatever clothes I had on? And what would I say to Marie-Claire if she were to wake up suddenly and ask me what I was doing?

So many questions rushed to my mind, but the state of arousal I had reached left no room to look for answers. It was too late. Every instinct in me was aroused. I was afraid of nothing by then; and nothing else mattered except that I get on with it, there on the bed, near her, and at once.

I heaved my body closer to her; I extended my head in her direction. I stared at her naked body, imagining it hot, relaxed, and wet with sweat. When I felt that I had looked at it enough and that its image in that aroused, seductive state was implanted in my imagination, I closed my eyes as I always did when I masturbated, so that the image I had captured would not escape me and I would be able to remain focused on the body I longed for. I then stimulated my nose so that it could detect and collect as much as possible of the scents of Marie-Claire . . . . I left it to God and went ahead.

The whole exercise lasted no more than a few seconds. I stifled my moans and shook with pleasure. Then I calmed down and my whole body relaxed. I remained motionless. After a little while I opened my eyes and looked at Marie-Claire to make sure that nothing had changed during those few moments when I had lost all awareness of my surroundings. As usual I felt guilty, but this time I did not care.

22

I had not seen her in three days.

I would go home late and find her sleeping, and in the morning when I awoke she would already have left the flat. It was obvious that she had started avoiding me just as I had started avoiding her. Previously, I would see her almost every morning, because the noise she made as she moved around in the living room, had her breakfast, or watered the plants, would wake me up. Sometimes she would look at me half smiling, or she would say something about the weather as if talking to herself. But for the past three days, nothing had been causing me to wake up. I would stay sleeping as long as I wanted. I don't know how she managed not to make a sound because she hadn't changed her habits, except I discovered that she now had her breakfast in the kitchen.

I left the hotel before the end of the shift, contrary to what was usual. Meloud, the hotel owner, did not hesitate one moment when I asked him if I could do so. No doubt he knew that it had something to do with my relationship with Marie-Claire. It was obvious to everyone at the hotel that it had deteriorated over the past few months. But instead of walking in the streets until late, as I had begun doing of late, I went home, driven by a sudden urge that created turmoil within me at a time when I thought I was immune to such things. A strange mixture of a longing to see Marie-Claire's face with a longing to know what she got up to at home at that time of day came over me; added to that was the slight fear that I may have overdone my absence.

As soon as I left the station, I took big strides. I wanted to reach home before her. I wanted to be the first thing she saw when she opened the door and entered, even though I was no longer certain that she still liked to find me home when she came back from work and that this gave her some comfort.

I stood in front of the door to the flat and listened, but I heard nothing. As I opened the door I feel mildly happy, a feeling that grew as I walked around the apartment and did not find her. I sat on the sofa. I started imagining everything she might say or do, and all the emotions that might be reflected in her face when she saw me.

I did not notice how much time had passed as I was immersed in my thoughts. When I looked at the clock on the stereo player I realized that it was a whole hour past the time when Marie-Claire usually came home. That did not surprise me, for she was not using the motorbike that I saw parked at its usual place in front of the building. This happened sometimes, especially if she was tired, because driving a motorbike in a city like Paris requires a lot of concentration and attention. The bus she was on was probably making its way now through the traffic that overwhelmed the city at that time of day.

I went back to imagining Marie-Claire as she discovered me in the flat. What surprised me this time round was that the more I dwelled on that idea the more I was certain that her reaction would not be a good one, or at least it would not be what I expected. "Nothing of what I expect will happen," I said to myself. "She will stop for a moment when she lays eyes on me, not as an expression of joy, of course, but of complete astonishment. She will wave her hand, nod her head or say something to greet me. She may ask me about the time I got home. She may even smile at me. That is all there will be to it. She will then leave me alone in the living room and immerse herself in her little chores."

Strangely enough, thinking of all that did not spoil my mood or diminish the feeling of happiness that had come over me since I had entered the apartment. What I truly wanted was to see her face after a long absence, and to know what she did during such a time. The only thing I wanted of her at that moment in time was for her to come home, as soon as possible.

Something I had not thought of before suddenly occurred to me. What if she ignored me completely? What should I do if she tried to humiliate me? What if she expressed her obvious repulsion, hatred, or resentment of me? What should I do if she stopped speaking to me, criticized me harshly, or mocked me? Would I be able to remain calm and collected? Would I be able to tolerate all these insults while waiting for the storm to pass?

I realized for the first time that the game I was playing might turn into a deadly trap, into which I would be the first to fall. But I did not care; the need to meet Marie-Claire was so strong that such questions, based only on assumptions, did not have the power to free me from this need or even to diminish its effect.

My body was relaxed from all that sitting, so I lay down on the sofa. And because I was afraid of falling asleep, which happened at that time of day when I was tired, I kept my eyes wide open and began contemplating my surroundings. I noticed that the plants had become little trees, and that her older plants had grown, becoming taller than the others. I also noticed that Marie-Claire had made small changes to the living room that I had not noticed before and which made me feel that things at home were getting out of my control. Small changes, but changes that implied to me, during these tricky waiting moments, that the house was no longer mine, and that Marie-Claire, who was always so careful to consider my opinion about everything, was somehow challenging me by making these changes without asking my approval.

I turned my attention to the paintings on the wall to relieve myself of these thoughts. I gazed at them, contemplating them one by one, starting with Marie-Claire's impressionist paintings. Once I was done, it occurred to me that rearranging them on the wall could reveal something new that we had not noticed before. I liked this idea, so I clung to it. Gradually I got so excited by the idea that I wondered if I might use it by suggesting it to Marie-Claire whenever I felt she was avoiding me or was refusing to talk to me.

Another hour passed by, but Marie-Claire did not appear. I thought of all the possible reasons for this delay; I remembered that she sometimes went to the supermarket nearby on her way home to buy some things and that she sometimes found it hard to get out because of the long queues at the checkouts.

I found myself once again compelled into imagining the awaited meeting. This time all my efforts were directed at her appearance and her clothes. I do not know why I imagined her thinner than before, that she had cut her hair, was wearing eyeliner, and beautiful clothes of vibrant colors. Maybe that is because I had a feeling deep inside that was trying to tell me she was about to change her life; maybe, also, because my need to see her after a long absence caused me to endow her with a little mystery so that she would be more desirable and that our meeting would be more satisfying.

I went back to my previous position without leaving my place; I extended my hand subconsciously to the small table near the sofa on whose lower shelf Marie-Claire piled the magazines she bought. I took one and flipped through it, focusing all my attention on the images and the advertisements. I looked through another magazine, then a third and a fourth. The more magazines I flipped through, the faster I turned the pages until I could no longer see all the images and advertisements in the last magazines.

I then moved on to the latest fashion catalogs Marie-Claire had received. I did not see it at first because it was under the pile of magazines. Usually Marie-Claire did not keep this kind of promotional publication, which she received for free. Sometimes she would throw them in the bin without flipping through them or even giving them a cursory glance. She did not hate fashion, she would say, but she did not understand all the attention it got. What also truly bothered her was receiving things she neither asked for nor wanted to receive; things created purely for the purpose of promotion and advertisement, and which were forced on people because they found them in their mailboxes every morning.

As I flipped through the smooth, glossy pages of the catalog, it struck me that a large section of it was devoted to underwear, and everything looked good on the models. Maybe that was why Marie-Claire kept this catalog; and maybe she hid it under the magazines so that I would not see it. "But since when has Marie-Claire cared about women's underwear?" I wondered, as I returned the catalog to where it had been so she would not find out I had discovered it.

I glanced quickly at the clock, which I was now avoiding; I was sure of what I was afraid of, and was trying hard to ignore—that the supermarket and other shops had long since closed. So, she is not there. She must have gone somewhere. Something important must have kept her from coming back at the usual time. I called her several times on her mobile. No reply.

"Don't worry yourself about that," I said to myself. "She won't be very late, for there is no reason that she should be. In a little while you will hear her footsteps as she approaches the door. Then you will hear the sound of the key turning in the lock, and the creak of the door as it opens. And suddenly, you will see her in front of you! Get a hold of yourself. Drive these fears and obsessions from your mind. Don't let anything deprive you of the pleasure of the anticipated meeting. In a little while, your wish will come true, and you'll see her face after a long absence. In the end, her reaction to finding you at home is not important. How she behaves toward you is also not important. This time it is enough that you just see her. That she is home with you. Don't pay attention to what you might not like about what she says or does. Be nice to her. Don't retaliate. Even if you feel that she's trying to insult you, if she quarrels with you or criticizes you, pay it no heed. Think of it all as trivial; make temporary use of the popular notions about women in your village, which, of course, you do not believe in, namely that women are airheads, who are not truly aware of what they say. That way you can remain calm, collected, and in charge of the situation. Also you must not forget that sooner or later she'll regret whatever she says or does. This regret may force her to apologize and ask for your forgiveness. This could be a good foundation for a new start to your deteriorating relationship."

I felt the urge to move. I got up and took a few steps as I looked around for something to do. But nothing in this house required tidying. I went into the kitchen to make sure that I had washed all the dishes and placed them carefully in the cupboard, for it made Marie-Claire happy to go into the kitchen and find it clean.

I went back to the living room, but I did not sit down: I stayed standing in the middle of the room, staring at my surroundings. I had to do something to help me bear the situation. Something pushed me to move. I wanted to make an effort to do something instead of just standing there like a pole with my hands tied or just lying on the sofa.

I noticed that a thin layer of dust had settled on the bookshelf. I got a wet rag from the kitchen. I ran it over all the shelves. I noticed a while later that the plant leaves had also gathered dust. That made me happy because removing the dust from the plants required a lot of time and effort and a great deal of care and attention. Also, Marie-Claire liked to see her plants at their best. I bent over one of them and got to work. From time to time I stopped to call Marie-Claire on her mobile, but she did not answer.

When I had finished cleaning all the leaves of the first plant, I took a break for a few moments and looked for a view of the plane tree.

I did not want to look around in the living room, so that my eyes would not fall upon the clock. I decided, as I moved to the second plant that I would stop looking at the clock all together until Marie-Claire returned.

But time passed and Marie-Claire did not return. Once it was past midnight I stopped cleaning the plant leaves and collapsed on the sofa. For the first time I thought of something that had not occurred to me at all—something I would not have believed had I thought of it earlier. She was not coming back home that night.

As I looked around me in astonishment I realized that everything I had done since I had got home had been useless. All the excitement at meeting her suddenly disappeared and was replaced with a sensation of pain combined with a strange sensation that seemed like relief. I no longer cared why she had not returned home, where she might be, or with whom at that late time of night. All my feelings poured into what my instinct was telling me, and my instinct was rarely wrong in such matters. My relationship with Marie-Claire was over this time; really over. And that was what happened. A few months later we got back together again and our relationship regained some of the serenity and joy of its earlier years; then we fought again. Marie-Claire spent another night away from home, then a third and a fourth. And one day, she left. She left with great ease. She left me with great ease, which I had not expected at all. This strange ease made me believe that there is nothing more fragile than the relationship between a man and a woman.

23

The living room is bigger and quieter without her.
It's been that way ever since that morning when she had carried off her plants and whatever I had failed to notice of her belongings still left in my apartment. She called me twice in the first weeks after she left to tell me gently and calmly that all my efforts to convince her to return to my home were in vain, because she no longer loved me and she could not imagine for a second living with a man she did not love. It is very important to her to be honest with herself and with others.

The truth is I was not surprised by her departure. In fact I believed she should have done what she did. I admit that I changed a lot after Marie-Claire spent her second night away from home. I started behaving badly and even violently at times, as if I wanted to drive her to leave the apartment and to abandon me.

I would lose my temper quickly and for the silliest reasons; for things like not finding my shoes in the morning where I had left them in the evening because Marie-Claire had put them in the right place, so that the bad smell they sometimes exuded would not spread to the living room and the bedroom, too. Or because, as soon as I opened my eyes in the morning, I found a cup, spoon, and knife on the table that Marie-Claire had neglected to take to the kitchen and wash, because she had had to leave the house quickly so as not to be late for work, which usually got her into a great deal of trouble. Or because I thought that the call with her mother,

164

who seemed in slightly better health, was taking longer than necessary, especially when I heard something that implied that her mother was talking to her about the weather in her village or something to that effect.

I also started blaming and reproaching her a lot. Sometimes I would criticize her harshly without reason and I would shout at her. And when she cried I would just look at her without saying a kind word as I had used to do—something to make her feel better and to indicate that I regretted what I had done. Or I would go to the bedroom and slam the door and turn the radio on loud so that I could not hear her crying, which aggravated me even more.

I started doing many things just to annoy and infuriate her; things that had never occurred to me before and that now seem amusing and ridiculous. I would not change my underwear every day. I would not spray my underarms with deodorant as she had taught me, especially as I did not believe that they gave off such a strong and horrible smell as Marie-Claire said. I would not cut the hair that she could clearly see inside my big nostrils, even though she had bought me a small pair of scissors especially for that purpose. I would not shave for several days because I knew she preferred to see me clean-shaven, as I am almost whiskerless, and in no way hairy, and what grows on my face is not a beard like that of most men but more like a goatee, as she would tell me teasingly. I also gave up the habit, which she had imposed on me, of changing my socks every day. That did not bother me at all, for I had known neither socks nor shoes until I was much older. Before that I had always been barefoot, which meant that I was always prone to stepping on thorns, rusty mails, and sharp stones, the scars of which can still be seen on the soles of my feet.

I also started to neglect household chores, which Marie-Claire had insisted we share from the moment she moved in with me so that she would not feel like a maid in her own home, as she used to say: taking the dishes to the kitchen after finishing our meal; washing them and putting them in the cupboard; cleaning the tablecloth when it was my turn; and cleaning the house, which I admit used to give me double pleasure as I pursued dust to the corners and all the hidden places, pushing the rubber tube of the vacuum cleaner everywhere.

But the straw that broke the camel's back was what happened when I came home drunk one late cursed night. I knew very well that Marie-Claire, who loved wine, got upset when she saw me drunk. She would say that drinking was an art, a joy, a celebration of life and its small pleasures. That was why people should not exceed the limit or else they would move from euphoric pleasure to drunkenness, which made them lose their reason and the ability to control their bodies. This was pitiful and pathetic. I also knew that it disgusted her to see me vomiting in the toilet, which happened sometimes when I got drunk, especially when I had had more than my fragile body could handle.

Nevertheless, I drank too much. I wanted to forget the nights that Marie-Claire had spent away from home. I had not slept well the previous night because of that, and from the moment I awoke I was tormented by questions because I couldn't continue deceiving myself, evading and analyzing the issue for fear of facing the truth. Everything within me rejected what I had tried to convince myself of for a long time, and that was that Marie-Claire had spent that night alone at a hotel to get back at me, or with some close friends whom she had not seen in a long while.

I took my time going back. I did not take the metro or the bus. I stopped at many bars that caught my attention on the way. I had a slow glass or two of Cointreau at each stop. I only decided to go home once I was sure that she would already be asleep. But I was surprised to find her sitting on the sofa in the living room when I opened the door. She was fully clothed. She had only taken off her shoes, and she had left them on the floor between her bare feet. She was sitting upright on the sofa, her arms crossed and her handbag in her lap as if she had just arrived. She was not doing anything. She was not watching television or listening to music. Everything around her was quiet in the dim light; she had only switched on the small lamp near the sofa. Had she come back only recently, contrary to what I had thought? And why had she not gone to bed yet? She had work the next day and had to wake up early as usual. Was she waiting for me? But why? Did she have something to say to me?! And what was the meaning of that look, which made me feel as though I were an alien from an unknown planet?

At first, I was at a loss as to what I should do. I did not know how to behave in this strange situation in which I suddenly found myself. A while later I was able to regain some control despite the bad state I was in. When she looked at me again, I put on a smile and sat down beside her.

"You stink."

I did not lose my temper. On the contrary I was somewhat relieved, for I interpreted her talking to me as a sign that she cared. A moment later she repeated her statement in a loud voice as she stared at me. I smiled at her once again because I was thinking as I looked at her lips, which I had not sucked on for a long time, of something that would not have occurred to me had she not spoken to me that way or stared at me so.

Should I agree with what she said about my smell—which I was not sure was true—just to prove to her that I would not lose my temper? I kept quiet for fear of any changes in her, or of her getting up, especially as I noticed that she had put her hand on the sofa near mine. I moved my torso back and

I started looking intently at her hand; it was wide open, the long soft fingers spread apart. But what caught my attention was that she was wearing nail polish. I had not seen them like that for a quite a while; and the deep red polish made her hands look more beautiful.

When I put my hand on hers and she did not withdraw it immediately as I had expected, I started wondering if she, too, had been thinking of what I had been thinking a moment ago. Moments later I started convincing myself of that, so much so that I imagined, in the state I was in, that Marie-Claire had not slept for that reason; that she was silently waiting for me.

And what was so strange about that? I asked myself with pride. Yes, what was so strange about Marie-Claire wanting me once again? "She knows very well what you can do for her. Has she not admitted on several occasions that you have taken her to cloud nine? She tried to move away from you. She tried to deprive herself and deprive you. But her body did not yield. No one can resist the urges of the body for too long. And there she is coming back to you. There she is waiting for you."

I came closer to her and I leaned over. When I put my hand on her shoulder, she said without moving or looking at me, "What a stench, you stink like your homeless friends."

I came closer still, and when I held her and tried to kiss her lips, she slipped out of my arms and pushed me away hard. Her reaction seemed strange, but I did not pay it much attention, believing it to be inevitable after everything we had been through.

I leaned on her again, and then I quickly lunged at her and started devouring her neck with kisses as I tried to get my hands beneath her clothes and between her open thighs.

"Leave me alone. Don't touch me."

I was determined to reach her lips because I knew that she could not resist for too long once I sucked her lips and moved my tongue inside her mouth, as she had taught me to do at the beginning of our relationship. I also wanted her as I never had before.

I enfolded her with one arm and pushed against her chest, pushing her into the arm of the sofa so that she would not be able to escape as she had done just a moment ago. I reached out my head as far as I could, searching for her mouth while I continued trying to caress her thighs with the other hand.

"Get away from me, I told you not to touch me. Don't you understand?"

I continued enfolding her and pushing nearer without a care for what she was saying or for the painful punches I was receiving on my back, my neck, and my forehead. When I finally reached her mouth and started kissing her lips passionately, I felt her relax beneath me. She stopped hitting me, pretending that she had surrendered to me.

When I moved my head back and started caressing her breasts, feeling the pleasure of victory and enjoying what was left in my mouth of the taste of her lips, she suddenly pushed me away. She leaned over me and started shouting, waving her open hands, which were shaking with anger:

"Do you want to rape me? I would never have thought you capable of that. What were you thinking? Did you think I would let you do that?"

I was determined to remain silent and not to answer her. But I don't know how I suddenly lost control. I got up and started shouting, too. We faced each other, hands waving in the air, and, as usually happened in such situations, we began swearing at each other.

Had it stopped there, we might have forgotten the insults with the passage of time, and we might have erased the effects of this violent fight the likes of which we had not known before, but what happened next destroyed any possibility of reconciliation and took our relationship to that point beyond which there was no return.

After a while, we stopped shouting and swearing at each other. I collapsed on the sofa, while Marie-Claire remained rooted to the spot. The moment she turned around to go to the bedroom, I suddenly get this strong urge to say something before she moved away, because it seemed to me that I had not sufficiently returned her last insult, which still rang in my ears. Without my being aware, she heard me say, in a low voice that seemed not my own, a few words which I do not know how or why came to my mind at that moment. And instead of speaking in French, I was surprised to find myself speaking in Arabic, "Qahba. Fajera." (Whore. Bitch.)

I had forgotten in my state of anger and drunkenness that Marie-Claire understood some Arabic words, especially those kinds of words. In all honesty, I had not even thought of that at all. She approached me as she repeated, "Kihba? Ana Kihba? Ana Kihba?"

The closer she got to me, the louder her voice became. When she picked up her shoe, I realized what an enormous mistake I had made, and that the words I had uttered had hurt her very deeply. I started saying as I moved back, "No, I did not say Qahba. I did not say Qahba."

But by now Marie-Claire was furious and incapable of hearing anything. She was moving toward me with great confidence, the hand holding the shoe raised up high and her eyes glistening with rage.

"Kihba? Ana Kihba?"

Fearing that she might hit me and that I might strike back in self-defense, thus making matters far worse, I ran to the kitchen. I went in and locked the door. I lay on the floor and replayed the incident in my mind as Marie-Claire uttered loudly, hysterically, and in broken Arabic, her voice hoarse from all the shouting, every swear word retained in her memory from the few trips she had taken with me to Tunis:

"Landeenummak . . . bara zamar . . . ya nayek . . . walid kihba." (Curses on your mother . . . go to hell . . . fucker . . . son of a bitch.)

I feel an urge to move, but my body does not obey. I remain on the sofa, looking around me in the large living room. For the first time since Marie-Claire left I think of moving my bookshelf back to where it used to be and putting the table exactly in the middle of the living room so that it will not look so empty.

I gaze at the plants once again and I see Marie-Claire bending over them. I see her putting the watering jug on the wooden floor to announce that she has surrendered herself to me. I see her bending down lower and turning her head a little so that her hair touches the freshly watered plants.

The place is empty and lonely now. There is nothing except a barely visible, thin layer of dust, and some marks on the wooden floor left by the heavy ceramic pots. I moved the only plant Marie-Claire left behind after leaving me: from the window to a corner in the living room, waiting to find the courage to throw it away. I found out very quickly that I am useless at looking after such delicate things for long.

I notice as I look at it that I have not watered it for some time. I get up and walk toward it. I decide, as I feel the leaves, which have started to wilt and dry, that I will water it later, once I have gone to the kitchen to prepare dinner. As I collect the dead leaves scattered all over the soil, I recall that Marie-Claire always used to remind me of the name of the plant, because I kept forgetting it, as it was an unusual name that I always felt was more suited to a wild animal than a beautiful plant such as this.

I stop collecting the dead leaves and I clear my mind of all passing thoughts so that I will not be distracted. I focus on the name of the plant that Marie-Claire gave me. I try for several long moments to remember it, but I cannot.